MARKET STREET CINEMA

MICHELE MACHADO

For Lisa.
I wish you would have reached out to me.
I hope you are finally at peace.

ACKNOWLEDGMENTS

Enormous thanks belong first and foremost to the ladies who unabashedly shared their experiences—the good, the bad, and the ugly—over cups of tea and trash TV.

To Stacy, who always reaches higher and remains a dear friend.

To Tanya Billey, for breaking the monotony with comic relief, long lunches, and an outlet for historical fangirling.

To Leigh Hogan, whose expertise and constructive criticism were essential to the editing of this manuscript.

And lastly, to Jessica, Christina, and Kenny, who know all my secrets and still love me for myself, and in spite of myself.

CHAPTERS

CHAPTER ONE

San Francisco Bay Area, 1998

My parents couldn't know about this. Not yet. With a love for history and a knack for fluffing my way through tests, I'd felt so sure I had what it took to pursue a higher education. Then laziness settled in. Once I began skipping classes, the usual excuses ensued:

> *I don't feel well.*
> *We're not really studying anything anyway.*
> *I'll go tomorrow, and it'll be like I didn't even miss a day.*

Unlike high school, where attendance was mandatory, the professors at Chabot didn't take attendance or assign homework. Virtually all grades depended on exams. My knack for testing failed me, or rather, I failed myself. In high school, the forced attendance ensured I absorbed enough material to score decently on a test. That didn't work so well for me in college. I drew a blank when I sat down to test, and I failed my exams.

After six weeks, I was a college dropout. It wouldn't have been so embarrassing if it had been a university; at least then, I could have chalked it up to being overwhelmed. But I had dropped out of Chabot, a community college that the students lovingly referred to as *Cha-blew-it.* And I *Cha-blew-it* in a big way.

I wouldn't be a history professor, an archivist, or a museum curator. It wasn't devastating, but it was painfully confusing. Those doors were now closed to me, my future path shattered with no discernible direction after a massive upheaval. I needed time to figure out what to do with my life, so while my parents thought I was in class, I was asking for more hours at my part-time job.

"I can up you to forty hours a week, but it will be mostly afternoons," Amelia said. She was born in Mexicali,

Mexico, and despite having lived in California for over thirty years, her accent remained thick. She picked up a pair of fuchsia panties, folded them, and added them to her stack.

My heart sank. I'd have to find another way to spend my mornings. "I'll take evenings then. I really need the hours."

Amelia nodded and carried on folding without looking at me. Her second chin bobbed with her head, and she pursed her thin, pink lips. "You haven't been here very long, but you're a good employee. You might have a future with Mod if you really want one, Lita."

Her compliment stung. I wasn't sure how a future at Mod Unmentionables might pan out for me. I had just gone from having sky-high dreams of a white-collar career to a lifetime of peddling lingerie in the mall. The store was a fun place to work, making the post of even a sales clerk on the lowest rung coveted. Still, I had too much pride to accept a career in retail as my destiny. Even if I were too lazy to achieve it, I had a yearning for something bigger.

Yet curiosity forced me to take the bait. "What kind of a future?"

"Sandra doesn't sell nearly the volume you do, and at some point, I'm going to have to promote one of you."

I tried hard not to giggle at that. Mod might have been a huge company with stores in every mall in America, but it was no Victoria's Secret. This location could only support Amelia, Sandra, and me. After six years, Sandra was still in the same entry-level position I was, but she at least displayed loyalty to the company. If that wasn't rewarded with a promotion, what could a nineteen-year-old with two months on the job expect?

"Why hasn't Sandra been made assistant manager yet?"

Amelia looked around the empty store cautiously before answering. "The company has no interest in promoting employees who don't want to move up. Why would I groom an assistant manager who isn't interested in eventually running her own store? If you tell me you want to be a manager and I promote you, it is better for Mod as a whole. They keep opening new stores and need them to be run by motivated employees."

"That makes sense, actually." My gaze remained on Amelia, and I studied her with a fresh layer of respect. She definitely understood Mod's business model. "How much does a store manager make?"

Amelia smiled and glanced at me out of the corner of her eye. "Are you asking how much I earn?" She was teasing me, of course, in her habitual, motherly way.

"Would you tell me if I was?"

"I would not," she said, chuckling. "The starting salary isn't impressive. It's under forty-five a year, but the bonuses and benefits are good, and if you prove to be an exceptional manager, there's always the chance of moving up to a corporate position."

"Forty-five is still better than minimum wage," I conceded. For half a second, I considered what she had said before the realization of how long all this might take overwhelmed my thoughts. "How long have you worked for Mod?"

"Twenty-six years. I started just like you—as a salesgirl."

Twenty-six years. Twenty-six years of folding overpriced panties and fixing colorful bras onto tiny hangers. That was a long time to be dreaming of a desk job at Mod's New York corporate office.

"Is there any way to fast-track that?"

Amelia chuckled. "Get a degree." She met my eyes, making us both burst out laughing. "I'm serious! You're young! I wish I had."

I released a sigh, propping my elbows on the counter, and buried my face in my hands. My hair fell forward, just long enough to tickle my elbows. I pushed the unruly brown locks away. "I know, Amelia. I really just can't. I don't have the discipline to get through it. I know I didn't try hard enough, but I know me. I would go back just to drop out again. I'm not college material. I wish I was, but I'm not."

Amelia patted my shoulder gently and allowed her hand to rest there. "I understand, Lita. College isn't for everyone. I'm not telling you that throwing in the towel after a few weeks is the best choice, but you're young enough to take a break and go back if you find yourself ready later."

I appreciated her support—I really did—but I knew I wouldn't be going back to Chabot or any other college. My prospects, whatever they were, felt elusive and empty.

CHAPTER TWO

"What were you thinking, dropping out of college?" Dad released the letter from his raised hand.

I watched it float back and forth in what felt like slow motion until it landed gently on the countertop. I could see the Chabot letterhead, so I knew what the rest said without looking. I also had a copy of that confirmation from the registration office. I wasn't expecting them to send a duplicate to the house. Had I known, I might have intercepted it, buying myself a little time.

Mom stood to the right of my father, her face betraying sadness so deep that it nearly broke my heart. "You have to go to college, Lita. What else will you do?"

I stood mute with my mouth dry, my mind searching for possible excuses. I was the queen of spin, but, somehow, I couldn't find the words to appease my parents.

My mother's eyes, glassy through a sheen of unshed tears, continued to question me silently.

"Can I take some time off to decide?" I swallowed hard, waiting only for steam to release from my father's ears.

His usually light complexion turned redder by the second. "You've already dropped out of college! If you wanted time to decide, you should have talked to us first. We might have been all right with you going part-time, but you withdrew entirely on your own!"

He spoke to me like I hadn't spent nearly every day of my life with him. As much as I would have loved to believe my father might have worked with me on this, I knew there was no way he'd have allowed me to go to school only part-time. It was all or nothing with him, just like it was all or nothing for me. I was a near mirror image of this man in both my looks and stubbornness. "I can't do it, Daddy."

"You won't do it. You didn't give yourself enough time to say that you can't do it."

"No," I fired back firmly. The initial shock of the unexpected confrontation began to ebb, and I felt the same resolution pounding in my head that had persisted when I made up my mind to leave school. I loved my parents. I respected them and wanted to placate them in most things. This I knew I couldn't bend to. "I can't do it."

"You will!" The words thundered from his lips. "You will because you're a smart girl, even if you've made a ridiculous, short-sighted decision!"

"It's mine alone to make, Dad!" My voice trembled but my determination held. I looked to my mother for help. I could usually find support in her corner, even though she rarely contradicted my father outright. She had her own method of channeling his obstinacy onto a smoother course. "Mom?" I pleaded weakly.

"Lita, please—!" she started, then burst into tears.

Dad wrapped his arms around his sobbing wife. He dipped his nose onto the top of her curly bob, whispering something I couldn't make out before turning back to me. "You have to finish college, Lita. This isn't a choice." His voice was still gruff, but his tone softened slightly. "I'm telling you, there's nothing out there for you without a degree."

"I love you, Daddy, but I've made up my mind. If I go back, I will just drop out again. I have to figure this out myself."

His jaw clenched, and anger flashed once more across his face. "You're better than this, Lita. You can do so much with your life, but instead you're going to throw it all away."

I lifted my chin defiantly. For the first time, I wasn't afraid of what he might say. I wasn't going to back down. "I'm not throwing everything away just because I don't want to go to college. I want to go in a different direction."

Dad released an exaggerated guffaw, letting go of my mother and pressing his hands onto the countertop. "And what direction is that?"

"The one that doesn't have me in a classroom for four more years." A condescending response, I instantly regretted it, even if it rang true.

He leaned in, the pressure on his hands turning his flaming knuckles and fingertips white. "That path usually leads to a lifetime of flipping burgers."

His cynicism didn't surprise me. He'd grown up without a mother and was frequently quick to remind me how lucky I was to bypass the struggles he'd faced. Stories

14

of him working nights at a shipping yard in Alameda so he could pay his way through college were repeated periodically. I wasn't entirely naive to the fact that my upbringing had been the exact opposite of his, and where he had to slave away to achieve his dreams of a university degree, the opportunity for the same education was being served up to me on a silver platter.

"Is that where you see me in ten years, Dad? That's all you think I will be able to do?"

"I think you can do anything you want, Lita. The problem is you're not willing to put in the work required to get your foot into a respectable door."

I bristled at his narrow idea of what doors might be considered respectable. "Give me a chance to figure it out, Dad. I might surprise you."

"Oh, you've sure as hell surprised me!" He lifted a hand and ran it through his salt-and-pepper hair, gripping a fistful tightly before slapping the counter.

"Just tell us what you're going to do," my mother begged. Her voice quivered, once again on the brink of weeping.

I didn't know the answer, but with a little time—

"I'll tell you what she's going to do!" Dad shouted, interrupting my frantic search for an answer. "She's going to get out there and start her life!"

I stood still, unable to comprehend his meaning.

"And if you're starting your life, it means you will be working full-time and living on your own. That's how real life goes. " His words struck me, the lightning to his thunderous tirade.

Mom let out a sobering whimper.

"Are you saying I have to move out?"

He didn't skip a beat. "That's exactly what I'm saying."

I opened my mouth to respond, but nothing came out. I was stunned into silence by both the harshness of his words and the sinking suspicion that I wouldn't be able to soften his resolve.

"I think a dose of reality might be just what you need to see how lucky you've been. I love you, Lita, but this is for your own good."

CHAPTER THREE

Tを to her word, Amelia scheduled me for a
forty-hour week. Between stocking edible
panties, cleaning out dressing rooms, ringing up
customers, and random bursts of tears, I scanned the
room-for-rent sections of local newspapers to find
affordable housing. The pickings were slim. It was no
secret that the San Francisco Bay Area was among the
most expensive places to live in the country, and I had
quickly determined there was no way I could get a whole
apartment to myself—or even share one with a roommate.
After calculating my earnings against the costs of car
insurance, gas, and a meager allotment for food, what
remained for rent left me too strapped for utilities. I didn't
even know what utilities would actually cost, but if they
were more than zero, I couldn't afford them anyway.

Thankfully, most of the room rentals included all utilities, except cable, which I could learn to live without.

The realization of how fortunate I had been to have parents who paid for absolutely everything didn't escape me, and in moments of weakness, I reconsidered my stance on going back to Chabot. They dissipated almost as soon as they appeared. If I reenrolled, I would just be prolonging the inevitable, and it really was time for me to try forging ahead on my own. I had to swallow all self-doubt and plow forward.

It didn't help my cause that I was too haughty to look outside the cocoon of the nicer cities in the area. I could comfortably rent a room in Hayward or San Leandro, but I kept my eyes on Pleasanton, Dublin, Livermore, and Castro Valley. San Ramon and Danville were too expensive, and anywhere else was too far away for my gas budget. From those few affordable listings, I made calls to schedule viewings, but my inquiries were frequently met with news that the rooms had already been snapped up or required a rental reference. My parents didn't count as a reference since I paid no rent. It felt like my prospects were being clipped before I even had the chance to test them.

Since most people with rooms for let were homeowners living in the house, they didn't run credit checks like the big property managers. Instead they counted on a bank balance with at least a couple months' cushion. Thanks to a twelve-hundred dollar high school graduation gift from my grandparents, I had that cushion covered.

I unearthed all these practices as I went along; my newspaper pages marked sparingly with red circles that were then crossed out with a heavy X.

"I'd like to return this." A pink negligee landed on my paper. I lifted my gaze from the classifieds to a late thirty-something woman with platinum hair and red lipstick. Her make-up was a little heavy for an early afternoon, but she still looked stunning.

"Is there something wrong with it?" I picked up the baby-doll to find the tag was still attached.

"It's not ripped or anything, if that's what you're asking. It was a present, but it's a little too sweet for my taste." Her heavy purse thudded on the retail counter, and she began to dig through it. "I think I have the gift receipt in here somewhere."

While she dug, I inspected the garment carefully, looking for any blemishes or signs of wear. The most telltale proof that the lingerie had been worn was what we lovingly called a *snail trail* in the crotch, and people attempted to return underclothes containing trails with disturbing regularity. "This looks okay for return. It hasn't been on sale since it came out, so I don't need a receipt if you're fine with store credit."

The woman smiled and glanced quickly around the store. "I'll pick out something else then."

"Is there anything in particular you have in mind, miss?" I had learned early that politeness paid off in sales, and if I was going to be stuck at Mod for the foreseeable future, I needed my sales to soar.

She crinkled her nose. "Oh, please don't call me miss. It's Darcy."

"Is there anything in particular you have in mind, Darcy? A certain look you're partial to?"

Darcy's smile turned into a wide, mischievous grin. "Small and sexy."

"That doesn't rule out a whole lot, I'm afraid. Everything in this store is sexy, and almost everything is small."

"What I mean is, no bra and pantie sets, and nothing too complicated." Her eyes wandered to a display of American flag-themed outfits along the opposite wall. "Those are perfect!"

Disappointment mounted as I followed her to the rack. The flag theme was on clearance, and I wouldn't get credit if she picked a red tag item. Darcy reached her hand up and grabbed a wet-look tank dress from its peg. The mini dress boasted a blue-and-white star print top, and a white-and-red striped bottom. "This is perfect for a girl named Liberty."

"It certainly would be, if you're shopping for a girl named Liberty."

Her hand waved my words away dismissively, and she laughed, leaning in. "I'm Liberty," she whispered.

I wasn't sure why she felt the need to whisper when we were alone in the store. I also didn't know what the hell she was talking about, as it had hardly been a moment since she'd told me her name was Darcy. "I'm sorry, I thought you said your name was—"

"My real name is Darcy," she interrupted, "but my stage name is Liberty."

Amelia had mentioned that the rotation of costumes and racier lingerie we sold made Mod a popular store for strippers and escorts, but that was mostly in the

San Francisco locations. My curiosity piqued, I decided to play dumb. This could be interesting. "Your stage name?"

She turned the hanger around to glance at the back of the dress, then draped it over her arm. "I'm a dancer at a club in the city. At Market Street Cinema. You heard of it?"

I hadn't, but for some reason I lied and nodded my head yes.

Darcy stepped back, slowly looking me up and down. "Do you get an employee discount here or something?"

It was a brazen query; hinting at a desire to mooch off of a stranger's employee discount. "I do but not on clearance items."

Darcy raised a single, pencil drawn eyebrow and released another laugh. "Not for me! I was just thinking about how these outfits would sell at the club. People come in sometimes and sell costumes, so if you brought in a few pieces bought at discount, you could probably sell them for full price on the spot. It would sure save me from having to come in here when I'd rather be sleeping."

It sounded like an amazing idea, but I couldn't help being skeptical. "I wouldn't even know what to bring or what sizes. I don't know anything about that." Well, I did know something about it. I knew it would look suspicious if I bought a pile of fetish lingerie in all different sizes, especially since only Amelia could ring up the employee discount.

Darcy poked a long, cherry-red fingernail into her coif and scratched her head. "Do you have catalogs?"

"We have catalogs, yeah."

Her eyes lit up. "Come by the club tomorrow and bring a catalog. You can pass it around the locker room and get an idea of what the girls want. Then, maybe come back the day after with some stock."

I was stunned by the invitation and, while unsure of how I could pull it off without being fired, I was interested enough to at least scope it out. "I could do that." I then remembered I had no clue where the club was. "Market Street Cinema, you said?"

Darcy's eyes narrowed playfully. "You've never heard of it before, have ya?"

I couldn't lie about it anymore, at least not to a woman who was extending an invitation that, if it actually panned out, might help supplement my income. My face felt like it was burning up. "I'm so sorry. I don't know anything about it," I admitted, embarrassed at being called out.

"No worries," she replied. "Just help me find some white gloves and panties to go with this get-up, and I'll tell you how to get there."

CHAPTER
FOUR

The heavy smell of tobacco and patchouli enveloped the entryway to the Market Street Cinema and clung in a haze along the polished brass handrails and burnt-red carpeting. Muted, pulsating music thrummed from a closed off area with bulky, movie theater-style doors. They opened briefly, and a young brunette woman in stilettos and a shiny lavender bikini disappeared around a narrow corridor. I stood, like a deer in headlights, next to a wall lined with gold-framed posters showing off scantily clad, busty ladies in all manner of sexy poses. It was ridiculous of me to be so startled, particularly when I clutched a catalog in my hand containing photos not terribly unlike the ones on the wall. Still, there was a separation between the catalog girls and me, while the poster ladies were probably wandering the halls of this club.

"You coming in or no?" The gruff voice rumbled over the vibration of the music, carried from behind a massive red-and-black circular podium.

"I'm...yes." Why was I hesitating? I shook my trepidation away and took a deep breath—a mistake, I realized, when I nearly gagged from the thick aroma.

"You here for a job?" The man craned his neck so his shiny bald head jutted over the podium. His Russian accent now seemed peculiar against his angular Arabic facial features.

I cleared my throat and raised my eyes to meet his. "I'm here to see Liberty."

"Liberty isn't working here tonight. She's at the Century. You want to talk to Mark?"

His words gutted me. It had taken nearly an hour to drive here, and parking had been a nightmare. I might have lived my whole life in the Bay Area, but all the trips I'd made from the suburbs to the city had been as a passenger, not a driver. The last thing I wanted to do was go back out onto the streets of San Francisco in search of another club. This left me with little choice. "Yes, please," I answered slowly. "I'd like to talk to Mark."

26

He nodded and picked up a black phone. From where I stood, his stare, fixated on me, revealed nothing beyond a hint of boredom, as a string of rapid-fire Slavic poured from his lips and into the mouthpiece. The theater door opened again, and a skinny woman emerged, tucking a wad of folded bills into a wristlet that dangled from her slender arm.

"Lotus!" At the sound of her name, the woman jerked her head up from the tiny purse and toward the podium. Her black hair swayed like a beaded curtain, its thick, blunt bangs framing a pair of heavily lined, almond eyes. "Take her down to Mark."

Her gaze met mine, and she began to walk slowly toward me. Each step appeared to be a sultry, carefully choreographed movement; the motions of an experienced ballerina in six-inch platform heels and a micro-tube dress.

"Come now. I take you to him." Her clipped Chinese accent was a stark contrast to the fluidity of her walk, which continued as she glided ahead of me. With almost no thought, I followed Lotus past an ATM machine, looking about a decade too old to still be working, to a worn staircase. An arrow directed upward, illuminated by flashing neon XXX lights. "Porn movies upstairs," Lotus said, pointing before she turned a tight corner. "Mark's office downstairs." She rested her hands lightly on each handrail and began a slow descent into near darkness.

A sense of dread set in, and my hands grew clammy as I clutched the railings. Most of me worried about the possible consequences of going into the darkened basement of a strip club with a stranger, but a small part of me was also concerned about Lotus toppling headfirst down the steep, narrow stairs in her towering heels.

My mouth went cottony. "Maybe I should just—" The lights flickered on, triggered by either motion or my rising fear. I felt some relief when I saw that the bottom was not too far off and not nearly as cavernous as I'd imagined.

"Just couple more," Lotus called back, a little louder than necessary given I was only four or five steps behind her.

Once on the basement floor, Lotus pushed boldly through a lipstick-red lacquered door that stood ajar. I crossed the threshold with far less gusto than she, taking in the cramped office through a fog of cigarette smoke. Behind an oversized mahogany desk with chipped corners stood an olive-toned, mustached man in a crisp, pistachio dress shirt. A cigarette clung precariously between his lips as he offered Lotus a grin and opened his arms wide. When the small woman fell into them, they wholly enveloped her. He patted her head like a favored child, winking as she pulled back from the embrace.

"Zakir told me bring her down." Lotus rubbed her hand playfully against Mark's chest. "I go back to work now."

I desperately wanted her to stay but didn't know how to ask without offending Mark. Before I could muster even the lamest excuse, Lotus slipped out the door, closing it behind her.

Mark lowered himself into a worn leather executive chair. It creaked gently as he relaxed, pulling the cigarette from his lips with lanky fingers burdened by heavy gold rings. "What can I do for you, miss—?"

"Lita." It came out barely above a whisper. My heart palpitated in near unison with the pulsing of the music above us.

"Lita," he repeated, nodding approvingly. He took a slow drag from his cigarette. "What can I do for you, Miss Lita?"

I pulled the catalog from my armpit, the seam moistened lightly by my sweat. "I came looking for

Liberty. I work at a lingerie store and thought some of the girls here might like some of the stuff."

He arched a thick, unruly eyebrow and released a draft of smoke. "And you do this as a representative of the company you work for or to make money for yourself?"

The question lingered in the air, mixing with his cigarette smoke. I couldn't lie, but I also couldn't tell the whole truth. "Both, I guess. I mean, I'll make something on a mark-up, but I still have to buy it through them." The words came out too quickly, and I knew they didn't sound convincing.

Mark chuckled, leaning forward in his chair. "And this was Liberty's idea? It sounds like something she'd cook up."

The last thing I wanted was get Liberty into any kind of trouble. I had no qualms about lying to prevent that. "No, it was my idea. I came in looking for her, hoping she might be able to help set me up. She's just a customer who said other girls might like the stuff."

With a wave of his hand, he brushed the answer away as if it didn't matter. "You're happy with the money you make at your store?"

"Not really. But is anyone ever totally happy with the money they make?"

Mark let out a throaty laugh, wagging his finger at me. "Clever girl, you are!" His laughter was interrupted by a hoarse smoker's cough. He balled up a fist and beat it against his chest until the hacking stopped.

"Should I get you some water?" I could use some myself. My mouth was still dry, and the secondhand smoke was destroying my throat.

"No, no, no," he wheezed out. "I'm fine."

I didn't believe him, but I also didn't really care. I had come to see if I could sell lingerie, and I didn't have an answer. "If it's better for me to call or come back another time, I can."

He cleared his throat a final time. "That's not necessary. I'm not in the business of selling lingerie."

It was a blow I felt deeply. I really needed the extra money. "Liberty said there were other merchants who were allowed sell directly to the dancers. Is that not the case anymore?"

"I don't need a girl to sell lingerie, but I always need more dancers. I'm changing the rules for vendors right now. If you want to come in and sell you can, but you pay the house fee like everyone else...like the dancers do."

I rolled back onto my heels, confused. "A house fee?"

He tapped his cigarette against an overflowing ashtray. "The girls all pay a hundred-ten dollar house fee to work. You're signed up as a contractor and come in for one of two shifts...day or night. If you tip Zakir twenty bucks, you won't have to dance on stage. You can sit in the locker room and sell anything you want. I don't care, as long as the house fee is paid."

In disbelief, I stared at him through a puff of smoke until it broke up and faded away. "So, in order to sell lingerie, I have to be a dancer?"

"Yes and no," he replied, shrugging. "Tip Zakir and don't dance, then consider the house fee a commission to the Cinema. Call it whatever you want, but that's the only way this is going to work."

A sigh escaped my lips. Liberty had made it sound as if some real money could be made. It was worth at least a try. "What happens if I don't sell enough to cover the house fee?"

Mark's dark eyes met mine. He took another deep drag from what was left of his cigarette and exhaled slowly. "Then, you dance."

CHAPTER FIVE

The hubcap of my trusty old VW scraped against the curb as I hugged it to the sidewalk and yanked up the hand brake. I was never much good at parking, let alone on a slope. I picked up the scrap of paper I'd folded and tucked halfway into the ashtray, double-checking the numbers scrawled across it. They matched the address stenciled on the mailbox.

Please let this be good.

I didn't know what I was in for, having called half a dozen listings for places I could barely afford, only to be told they'd already been rented. If this didn't work out, I'd have to swallow my pride and rethink my willingness to live in less desirable areas.

I got out of the car, and the heavy door swung shut on its own. The incline of the street apparently affected more than just my parking skills. The driveway was also unusually tilted, but the raised front yard gradually leveled in front of a pear-colored house. A handful of cement steps led me to the front door, which I knocked on, perhaps a bit too tentatively.

My eyes wandered over the lawn, which looked like it had been recently mowed. Grass clippings lay atop the perfectly green stubble, except for two small patches that had scorched brown under the California sun. I loved the smell of fresh-cut grass. A breeze carried the soft jingle of wind chimes and a rustle from the palm fronds sheltering them in an obliging tree. Despite being squeezed among houses on both sides of a cramped residential street, this particular house felt like it had been picked up and moved from a more provincial setting.

I knocked again, louder.

A child squealed from somewhere on the other side of the door. *Someone's home, thank goodness.* With a swish of fabric, the blurry shape of a woman approached from behind a sheet of frosted privacy glass. *Click, clack.* The locks surrendered and the door lurched open.

"You must be Lita!" Her raspy, high-pitched words nearly bowled me over, and I took a half step back. She laughed, and her expansive body jiggled in unison. "Nothin' to be afraid of, honey! Come on in!"

She moved further inside, allowing the door to open wide enough for me to pass. I stepped over the threshold and onto a knoll of toffee-tinted shag carpeting. Two sets of stairs greeted me, one that went up toward a bright landing, and another that went down into what looked like a door to the garage. "The room is downstairs, but come on up for a minute."

Lifting the hem of her billowing kaftan, she ascended the stairs rather quickly for a woman of her girth. "I'm Patty, by the way. I know we spoke briefly on the phone, but I couldn't remember if I told you my name or not. I get so carried away sometimes!"

She hadn't said her name, but she did get a bit carried away on the phone. It had been less than a two-minute call, but Patty's excited rambling over such mundane details as her address had left me exhausted when I put the phone down.

"Nice to meet you, Patty." I meant it. For all her huffing and puffing and chatter, Patty seemed like a genuinely pleasant woman.

I followed my hostess into a large living room with impossibly high ceilings, decorated to the hilt with all that was fashionable in the late 1970s: a sofa suite and recliner made of tartan avocado upholstery, an assortment of lacquered walnut coffee and side tables, and a pair of wicker peacock chairs that looked out toward the fabulously manicured backyard. However heavy and dark the furnishings were, they were brilliantly offset by the glittering sunshine that filtered in through the floor-to-ceiling windows. That same bright sunshine made Patty's amber bouffant appear positively carrot-hued.

"This is my little slice of paradise," Patty said. Her eyes grazed over the room approvingly, then landed squarely back on me. Her brows furrowed. "You're a bit young. You can't possibly be older than seventeen or eighteen."

A wave of anxiety brushed over me, my hope of finding a place quickly diminished by her remark before I'd even seen the room. "I'm nineteen, but I have a reliable job and work full time." The words tumbled out a little too defensively. For all its quirkiness, this house was already so much better than I'd anticipated. "I work at the mall in Pleasanton. You can call my boss."

Patty stood perfectly still, taking me in with her eyes. Her brow remained crumpled. She was definitely trying to determine if I were being truthful or not.

"I need to find a place to live. I promise I can afford the rent and will be no trouble at all." Now I sounded desperate.

Patty's face softened, and her mouth widened into a smile. "What are you running away from, honey?"

I opened my mouth to respond, but nothing came out. I didn't know the answer to her question, because I wasn't really running. Right now, I was just floundering. Floundering, mouth agape, in front of an inquisitive woman who had a reasonably priced place to sleep. "I'm not—"

A solid *something* collided with my legs, and I hopped to the left to avoid being knocked to the ground.

"April, look out!" Patty shouted, bending over and scooping a chunky toddler up into her arms. She planted a kiss on the little girl's forehead. "April, say hello to Lita."

April waved a plump hand toward me, crinkling her nose and smiling.

"Nice to meet you, April," I said, grateful for the distraction.

Patty set her daughter down beside her. "She's not much of a talker. The doctors say she's on the Autism spectrum, but I'm not buying that just yet." While I was again left without a response, that didn't matter. Patty didn't look like she required one, nor did she leave much time for me to give one anyway. "It's just the two of us," she said. The smile never left her face. "It would be nice to have a young lady in the house, even if our paths don't cross much."

I was instantly flooded with relief. Perhaps there was hope still.

She squeezed my shoulder as she walked past to the top of the staircase. "Let me show you what I've got down there."

At this point, I wasn't terribly concerned with what I'd be shown. Virtually nothing available on the market was in my price range, and the few that were had been snatched up. I knew my dollar wouldn't stretch beyond a small hovel.

Patty twisted the knob on a wood-chip door at the base of the stairs, waving her arm dramatically as she entered. "Voila!"

It was...

I couldn't...

"This is the room you're renting out?" I asked, almost breathlessly. It wasn't actually a room. It was a rather generously proportioned studio apartment.

"More of a mother-in-law unit," Patty replied. She took clear pride in my surprise.

It wasn't huge, but it was certainly many, many times larger than I'd expected. It only shared the house's 70s theme in its wood-paneled walls but was otherwise pleasantly furnished with slightly more modern, neutral tones. "And this is renting for—?"

"Just as listed," Patty interrupted. "I need a little help with the mortgage. Utilities included. It isn't much, but it has everything you'd need."

It isn't much? I was certain Patty had placed her ad without any idea of what was out there. "It's perfect."

The studio was L-shaped, the main living space boasting a sofa and loveseat of ivory, and a twin daybed partially concealed behind a folding screen. There was a door ajar just beside a tall chest of drawers. "Is that the bathroom?"

Patty bobbed her head. "It is but it's tiny. That shower might look like it belongs in a camper, but it's still a full bathroom. Kitchen's just over here." She pointed to the curve of the L, where accordion paneling had been pushed flush against the wall. A microwave sat to the right of a small sink. A wood ledge held a toaster oven—just barely large enough to manage my love for baking. A double electric hotpot cooktop sat on the counter. "It's little but it's functional."

I was in a state of absolute disbelief. This place would eat up two-thirds of my wages but still leave the wiggle room I needed to pay all my other expenses. It would be tight, but I could actually do it. I just needed to convince Patty. "Do you have someone else interested in the room?"

It was a stupid question. Of course she had others interested in the room.

"The ad came out this morning, and I've had more calls than I could answer, but most were men, and you are the first to come look."

I turned to her. "You really can call my boss to check on my employment." The pleading tone was unmistakable. I didn't care. I was prepared to beg.

"Oh, puppet!" she cried out. "You look like a wounded kitten! How could I say no to that?"

The weight of a mountain lifted from my shoulders. I could barely breathe I was so relieved, but I still wasn't going to give her even a minute to change her mind. "Can I move in tonight?"

Patty took a key from the hip pocket of her kaftan and placed it on the little kitchen countertop. "Consider yourself moved in as of now."

CHAPTER
SIX

The first month's rent and deposit nearly cleaned me out. My checking account was bleeding to death, but I had a place to live, my car, a full-time job, and the Mod Unmentionables catalog to bring to the club tonight. Mark apparently told Liberty that I had come in, because a message asked me to call her back when I got into work the next afternoon. After a quick conversation, we agreed that I'd meet her today on platform two at the Castro Valley BART station. We'd take the 5:56p.m. train into San Francisco together. That sounded a hell of a lot better to me than trying to drive there again.

And now I waited.

The platform was practically empty, which made sense, considering the Daly City trains were running in the opposite direction of rush-hour commuters. When the ping of the intercom announced the arrival of the 5:56 train, I had still seen no sign of Liberty, so I walked quickly to the top of the escalator, hoping she'd be racing up it. The *beep-bi beep* of the approaching train punched through the air, and my hair lifted around my face as the first car pushed wind across the platform. I pulled my jacket tightly around me until the seams felt like they might burst. She wasn't there.

Goddammit.

I wasn't sure what to do. For all her good intentions, this was the second time Liberty had stood me up. The first time she wasn't where she said she'd be, I ended up signing a contract with Mark to be a blasted stripper. Now I was on my way back, to do who knew what.

Not to strip, that's for sure.

Why on Earth would I do that when, if I didn't make the house fee, I could just walk out the front door and never look back? That was why I'd signed. They don't arrest strippers for not paying a stage fee.

But I didn't want to go back there alone. I wanted to walk in with Liberty, who could at least introduce me to the girls and put in a good word for the lingerie.

The train came to a halt, and the doors opened. I had to decide if I was going to get on.

"Lita!"

I snapped my head toward the sound. Liberty stood in the doorway of a car, waving me toward her.

"Oh, thank God!" I shouted back to her, clearing two full car lengths at a pace faster than I'd ran in ages. I crossed over the thick yellow line and into the carriage just as the doors slid shut. "I didn't think..." I sucked down a gasp of air. "...You were coming! " I collapsed into the nearest seat. My chest felt like it might explode.

Liberty plopped down next to me, laughing. "You know, you could have just gotten on the first car and walked through to this one."

I was panting too hard to offer more than a shake of my head in reply.

She patted her cherry-red–tipped fingers against my knee. "Sorry if you thought I might not come. I got on at Dublin-Pleasanton."

I inhaled deeply, then exhaled heavily, trying to catch my breath. "That would have been good to know beforehand."

"I can be a little scatterbrained sometimes." She pinched the same knee she had just been patting. "Did you bring the catalogs?"

I reached into my black hobo bag and pulled out the sales books. "Got 'em."

"Have you figured out pricing yet?"

I tucked the catalogs back into my purse. "For anyone the same size as me, it'll just be retail. I can get away with buying my own sizes with my discount. Otherwise, I'll add a ten percent markup."

Liberty clicked her tongue. "You won't make more than a couple hundred dollars that way."

"A couple hundred dollars!" The hair stood up on the back of my neck. "I'll be thrilled with a couple hundred dollars."

"But after the stage fee, it might only be a hundred."

I couldn't believe what she was saying. Anything over forty dollars profit meant I'd be eating more than potatoes and ramen this month. "After I pay the stage fee and buy the lingerie, I hope to make sixty bucks. If I can do this maybe once a month, that'll really help me out. I just moved into my own place."

Liberty's eyes widened. "You are living on your own? No roommate or anything?"

It was an awkward thing, telling someone you were broke and didn't actually have any friends. "It's a mother-in-law unit, so there's a woman and her daughter that live upstairs. I'm not really alone."

"What about a boyfriend?" Liberty leaned into me, teasingly. "You're adorable. Don't tell me there isn't a man."

I pushed my shoulder back into hers. "Should I just say nothing, then?"

She belted out a loud laugh.

If the car hadn't been empty, I'd have probably been embarrassed. But for the first time in a long while, I was actually enjoying myself. I could afford to be a little more honest with the person responsible for that. "I had a boyfriend in high school, and we'd been together for about two years. Right after we graduated, my best friend—really, my only friend—got pregnant. It was his."

Liberty took a sharp intake of air. "You have got to be fucking kidding me!"

"If only I was." I rested my head back on the seat. It had happened almost six months ago, but it felt like just yesterday. My heart still hurt at the loss of two people I cared about. "I hope their baby is ugly."

"It's not the baby's fault!" She elbowed my arm.

"I know, I know. I hope the baby isn't ugly." I felt bad for saying such a shitty thing, even if I was half joking. Sort of. "What about you? Are you married?"

"I was married for a couple years, a long time ago. No kids. I'm getting old and won't be able to dance much longer, so I'm focusing on earning and saving right now. I want to open a little teahouse. A shop that serves tea with the usual sweet and savory nibbles and sells loose leaf. All kinds, from everywhere."

I was impressed that she had a plan and was genuinely happy for her. "That sounds amazing. You don't think you could open your teahouse with a husband in tow?"

Her eyes became liquid. *What was that? A hint of sadness?* "A man would distract me. Not that I could find a good one who wanted to take on a forty-four-year-old stripper."

"You don't look a day over thirty-five," I said, smiling. It was true. She didn't.

Liberty looped her arm through mine. We stared silently out the window, watching the suburban cities whiz past until we made it to our stop at San Francisco's Civic Center.

A free for all of naked women awaited me in the dressing room. I had never been shy about my body or changing in locker rooms, but this was another level completely. As far as I was concerned, Liberty's apprehension over how much longer she might be able to dance was wholly unfounded. Women of all shapes, sizes, and ages meandered the basement of Market Street Cinema in their birthday suits, applying make-up and using toilets without stall doors. Easily more than thirty women packed into the narrow, Z-shaped space.

A slender, muscular woman with a fading peacock tattoo sleeve secured the strings of her black bikini. "We got ten minutes 'til lineup."

"Fuck the lineup!"

I couldn't see who issued the reply but thought it probably slipped from the glossy lips of a strikingly beautiful dark-skinned girl in a cropped blond wig. She caught me eyeing her and examined me up and down. "Aw shit, we got a new girl."

A collective moan rumbled across the long row of women, who were all seated in succession before a vanity mirror that stretched from one end of the enclave to the other.

Liberty wrapped her arm around my waist protectively. "Calm down, ladies. She's not here to dance. She sells costumes."

Peacock Sleeve stood up, slipping her foot into a spiked stiletto. "I want one of those strappy slingshot sets. You got any of those?"

I knew exactly what she was talking about and pulled the catalog from my bag. "I have the two-piece style. A triangle bikini top with a g-string bottom. The pantie straps go over the shoulder instead of the hips."

"Let me see," she said, walking toward me with her arm extended.

I flipped quickly to the page and handed it to her. "It's forty-eight dollars." The slingshot was easy since it only came in one size. I had jotted my prices in the book earlier in the day while working at Mod.

Liberty peered over the woman's shoulder. "That would look hot on you, Swan."

Swan, with the peacock sleeve, handed the catalog back to me. "I'll take it in black. But I gotta go earn that forty-eight dollars first." She brushed past without another word.

"She's got catalogs and will be here until ten if anyone needs anything!" Liberty shouted.

I whispered to her, "Hey, I wasn't planning on staying until ten." I had hoped an hour or so would be sufficient.

"You have to. They're all going to be like Swan. They need to make the money first." She took the catalog from my hand and set it on the vanity. "Catalogs are here," she shouted. "Just write your name next to what you want and pay Lita before ten. She'll be back tomorrow with your things."

Back tomorrow?

"Oh, Liberty, can't I just meet you at the station again and you can bring them back?" I didn't really want to make two trips here. Every train ticket I bought cut into the little I hoped to make, and if Liberty were coming back to work tomorrow anyway...

"Girl, I live here in the city. I was in Pleasanton shopping because the stores are less crowded. I rent a one bedroom in Haight-Ashbury, right between the Haight and Cole Valley."

I went slack-jawed. "How the hell do you afford an apartment in the city?"

She began to undress, and I wasn't sure if it were more polite to look away or pretend I didn't notice she had just taken her pants off. I went with the latter. "I work here five days a week to make enough to pay my rent, my bills, and save for my shop. I do it, but it's getting harder." She pulled her panties off and exchanged them for a crisp white thong from her backpack. "I need to get ready for the lineup." The women were all filtering out and up the stairs.

"What's the lineup?"

Liberty pulled her top over her head, exposing a pair of plump breasts. She quickly tugged a worn white wife-beater tank over her nipples, which were barely covered by a hem that she'd jaggedly cut with scissors. "Seven o'clock is kind of the crossover time from dayshift to nightshift. Their quitting time is seven-thirty, so Mark has us all line up on stage at seven. It makes the men think there's a lot more girls than there really are, but they also get to see them all at once on stage."

"I don't really want to stay down here in an empty locker room." It felt creepy and kind of made me claustrophobic.

"I wouldn't," Liberty replied, flipping her head forward. She shook her hair, then tossed it back. The result was fabulously tousled and sexy. "The Market Street Cinema is haunted."

I looked around skeptically. "Shut up."

Liberty laughed. "That's what they say, but I've never seen or heard anything, and I've worked here for over ten years." She shoved her backpack into an obliging locker, slamming it shut and clicking her combination lock into place. "We've got to head upstairs to the club now. It's showtime."

I followed her up the stairs, keeping my eyes on the steps for two reasons. First, the incline rose so steeply that, even in flats, I could scarcely trust my balance. Second, Liberty sashayed up them, ahead of me at just the right number of steps to have her nearly-bare ass squarely in my face. "Where am I going? Not on stage, I hope."

"No, no...not on stage," she threw back over her shoulder. "Just sit in the audience. No one will bother you."

At the landing, we turned a sharp corner to emerge near the club entry. From our angle, I could see a couple of men lined up to pay Zakir, who stood post at his podium playing DJ and cashier to both the men coming in and the girls paying out. Mark might have been in charge, but Zakir ran the show.

"Through here," Liberty motioned. The disco music, which pulsed and vibrated throughout the building, turned to thunder when she pushed open the heavy theater door. "Sit anywhere, and I'll come find you after," she shouted.

It still looked like an actual theater. A black curtain hung between the heavy red velvet drapes at both sides of the massive stage, where two poles gleamed, one at each end. A catwalk extended halfway through more rows of seats than I cared to count. Full capacity exceeded two hundred and fifty, for sure. The illumination from the stage cast the men scattered throughout in silhouetted darkness. They were easy to count, eighteen black forms. The backstage entry sat to the right, while on the far left, open doors led to another section. Along the open walkway behind the seats, a padded black wall stood in near complete darkness. For a moment, I thought I saw movement against it but couldn't be certain.

I chose a seat in the last row, with my back to the walkway and its mysterious padded wall, and settled in. I felt ridiculous.

"Lineup in one minute!" I jumped as the loud, muffled words rang through the speakers. Zakir's unmistakable Slavic accent cut off with the shrill screech of feedback.

I didn't want to think about what manner of cooties thrived on the fabric seat I had chosen. My skin crawled every time I touched anything. They should really reupholster the theater seating in a non-porous, easy-to-disinfect material. Honestly, I just wanted to leave.

Then the floodlights on the stage began to change colors, purple and red crisscrossing, one over the other, to the rhythm of Vicki Sue Robinson's *Turn the Beat Around.* A small slit in the black curtain at the rear peeled open, and a line of mostly bikini-clad women in lucite platforms poured out. Black, white, brown, and Asian; tall, short, fat, and slender, there were so many women. Most appeared to be quite a few years older than me, but heavy make-up and the flattering effect of red lighting made it difficult to tell. Tiny wristlets dangled from one arm of each, the one accessory they all had in common.

"Destiny." Zakir sounded bored as the name crackled through the sound system.

A tall, fleshy woman in a metallic fuchsia skirt and bandeau emerged from the line. She prowled down the

55

catwalk with the confidence of a queen, then returned to her place in line.

"Fantasia."

From dead center, a leggy brunette in a white net micro-mini pulled from the line for her turn.

"Candy."

Another woman stepped forward, radiating dominance in black pleather and raven victory rolls that fought against skin so icy white, she seemed almost translucent.

"Allegra."

I tried not to giggle at choosing an allergy medication as a stage name. Pretty and edgy, I watched her in awe.

"Harmony."

A Hawaiian woman easily pushing fifty sauntered forward, her hair backcombed around her face creating a winged frame. She scanned the audience like she owned the place.

"Ember."
"Ireland."
"Porsche."
"Dolly."
"Willow."

Zakir droned on and on and on. With every call, a woman who oozed sex and certainty sashayed her way down the catwalk. It was a buffet of different looks and body types, a delicacy available in whatever flavor of lady one desired. While most of the women didn't meet the Hollywood ideal of beauty, they were each alluring in her own way. As every woman took her turn, I slowly shrank deeper into my seat, fascinated by the power they exuded and equally crushed by the weight of my own insecurities.

CHAPTER
SEVEN

"These are all for you?" Amelia asked, raising a single brow as I dropped the pile of lingerie on the counter.

"The ones in my size are, yeah." My eyes flickered everywhere but her gaze. I wasn't adverse to dishonesty when I had an empty refrigerator to fill, but that didn't make me any good at lying. "The other ones are gifts."

Amelia hooked her index finger through a lace crotchless pantie, lifting it. "This is a gift for someone?"

It was possible I hadn't quite thought this through as well as I had initially believed. My face felt hot. "Someone I know is having a bridal shower. She asked me to bring some naughty favors."

Amelia released the underwear. "And the ones for you?"

My cheeks felt on the verge of bursting into flames. "I don't know, Amelia. I got dumped a while back, and I've been feeling like crap ever since. I'm just trying to cheer myself up."

Amelia's face dropped, and her eyes turned downcast. "Oh, honey! I'm so sorry!" She reached her hand across the counter and squeezed mine.

Retail therapy might be a plausible excuse for anything, but making a woman who had always been kind to me feel guilty for asking legitimate questions—well, I was pretty sure I might go to hell for that. "Please don't be sorry." I pulled my hand back. "I'd just rather not talk about it."

Concern remained etched across her face, and she kept her eyes on me. My gaze hovered somewhere past her shoulder.

After what felt like an eternity, the chirp of the scanner broke the uncomfortable silence. Amelia was sifting through the pile in search of price tags. I reached in, separating anything in my own size.

"Thanks," I said, sounding sheepish.

Amelia smiled, not looking up from her task. "We all sometimes need a little pick-me-up. Believe me, I've been there. Although..." She shook her head and chuckled. "I tend to just buy ice cream."

I wasn't sure how much lower I could sink in this embarrassment. Having my boss think that I was buying a glow-in-the-dark g-string as a pick-me-up hit bottom-feeding territory. "I'll remember that for next time."

"I hope there isn't a next time," she replied.

I needed the money but knew I couldn't go through this again. "There won't be." It was the only honest thing I'd uttered so far.

Amelia gave me the total, and I quickly paid with my debit card, grateful I'd had the foresight to deposit the stack of crumpled, sweaty bills before coming in. She handed me the receipt. "Didn't you say your mom was going to meet you for dinner?"

I paused, forgetting for a moment that I'd mentioned that. "She was, but I called and asked if we could do it another time."

Amelia frowned. "Not really in the mood, I suppose."

"I know how it'll be. She'll just try to talk me back into college." I tucked the receipt in my handbag. I loved my mom, but I had to focus on me right now. I hadn't even given her my new home phone number yet, so she could only reach me at work. "I haven't spoken to her since I moved out."

Although I had told them I was going to find my own place, the move had happened so quickly that they were stunned by the abruptness of it all. It was evident that neither of my parents had actually been expecting me to go through with it. Now that it was done and they had stopped reeling, my mother was reaching out to talk. I had yet to hear from my father and didn't expect to. He was going to take longer to come around.

I added, "I need some time to settle in and figure out what I'm doing."

"And have you decided what you're doing?" Amelia asked, with concerned softness.

I picked up the bags. "Aside from dropping off some party favors? Not at all." I gave the bags a playful wiggle and turned to leave. "Thanks again, Amelia. I'll see you on Tuesday."

"Enjoy your Sunday and Monday, sweetheart," she replied, raising her voice as I got closer to the door.

"Thanks!"

I had made enough selling lingerie to get some proper groceries and not dip further into my savings, a huge relief. Now I just had to deliver them.

Zakir let me through with a wink, thanks to a highly effective pout and some mild flirting from Liberty.

"Are you sure I'm not going to come back up and be surprised with a house fee?"

"Not a chance," she responded. "Mark is dealing with some issue at the Century tonight, and Zakir doesn't care as long as he gets tipped."

I stopped in my tracks. "I can't tip him out again, Liberty. Even twenty bucks is a lot for me right now."

She continued down the stairs without so much as a glance back. "Stop worrying! There're girls here tonight that weren't here yesterday. You'll make some extra cash again."

I began to shuffle after her, clutching the bags to my chest, careful not to die in a tumble down those wicked stairs while delivering undies to strippers. "Can you please stop for a sec, Liberty?"

She was already at the landing, looking up expectantly. "What's wrong?"

I descended the last three steps in anxious haste.

"I can't buy anymore lingerie. I wish I could because I genuinely need the money, but my boss at Mod—it was just too weird."

Liberty flashed a wide smile. "There are other ways to make money."

"Don't be a bitch." I was out of breath and in no mood to mess around. "I don't know anything about dancing."

Liberty laughed loudly. "If all you're worried about is the dancing, you shouldn't be. The dancing is nothing. It's the hustle that's hard as hell."

I had no idea what she was talking about. "How can a stripper not worry about dancing? And what's the hustle?"

"Oh, girl, you are so very young!" She wrapped a bare arm around my shoulder and half-hugged me. "You're only on the stage for fifteen minutes. The rest of the time, you're in the audience trying to get private dances...which aren't even really dances. But you get them and make your money by hustlin'."

Based on what I'd seen the night before, I half understood what she was saying but didn't know how to respond.

"You came in here with the catalogs and hustled. It's the same thing out there." She removed her arm from my shoulder and looked me square in the eye. "But you shouldn't do it if you don't want to."

I had nothing against adult entertainment, so my mind raced. Curiosity and fear fought against each other. "It's not that I don't want to. I mean, I'm not saying *I do* want to..." Now I was confusing myself. "I just never considered it, that's all. I don't know anything about it."

"I'll tell you what," Liberty said, taking the bags from my hands. "Let's get these knickers to the girls who ordered them, and I'll take you out on the floor again after."

"I can't pay the stage fee," I reminded her.

"Don't worry about that. I told you, Zakir won't care." She lifted the bags and began to move through the locker room.

"I can't tip him either, Liberty!" It came out louder than I'd hoped.

She swung around, walking backward with her usual grin. "If he thinks he can get you in as a real dancer, that'll be tip enough…for tonight."

I held back as the women all swarmed around Liberty for their outfits. It was my third visit to the club, but I remained an outsider looking in. The distribution took all of five seconds before we were back upstairs, pushing our way through the heavy doors and onto *the floor*—as Liberty kept calling it.

There, a curvy Latina stretched on stage, completely naked, with her legs spread eagle. An older man leaned in as close as he could, his face less than a foot from her *va-jay-jay*. He slid a bill the rest of the way until his fingers grazed the inside of her thigh. She smiled at him and rolled over, pulling herself up and gliding to a pole.

"So, it's all fully nude here?" I had to shout above the music as I watched the dancer swirl effortlessly around the brass rod.

"That's the only reason you'd be able to work here," Liberty replied. "Fully nude clubs can't serve alcohol. Too dangerous. You only need to be eighteen to dance nude, but you have to be twenty-one if you just want to dance topless. It's so backward!"

I crossed my arms across my chest, self-conscious that there wasn't a whole lot there. It was unlikely I could charge high rent for anyone to park their eyes on my breasts, not when they had the choice between my boobs and Liberty's shapely set.

"It doesn't matter," Liberty said, resting her hand on my wrist. "You're young. They love young more than they love double-D's."

"How the hell did you—?"

"I've got a few minutes until lineup. Have a seat." She pushed me into one of the filthy audience seats, then sat on my lap. My instinct was to squirm, but I resisted. She leaned in, her breasts brushing against my chin. "You want a dance?" she whispered in my ear. Her voice was sultry, almost breathless.

I froze. I didn't know this Liberty.

"That's how you start!" she said cheerfully, pulling back. It was astonishing how easily she transitioned from one persona to another. "Ninety percent of the time they will say no, but once you get the hang of it, you'll get plenty of yeses too."

I swallowed, hard. "I don't think I would be able to do that, Liberty."

She tucked a stray hair behind her ear, leaning in again so she didn't have to shout. "If you want to give it a try, we can work together on Monday. But only if you want to."

Mistrust filled my head. She wasn't being pushy, but this entire conversation felt weird. "Do you get anything if work here?"

She pulled back abruptly, furrowing her brow and frowning. "Oh, Lita! No, honey! Oh God, no...Please don't think I'm selling you out!"

"I'm sorry, Liberty." I felt so unbelievably guilty. She'd been exceedingly helpful, even drumming up more lingerie business for tonight without anything in it for herself. "I just had to ask. I'm sorry."

Her face lit back up. "Don't be sorry. I've been in the game for so long, I don't think about what it was like in the beginning much anymore."

I sat quietly for a moment, the throb of music washing over like a wave. Based on the cash being counted and shoved into wristlets downstairs, I wanted to try. But I didn't have an ounce of the confidence Liberty exuded— that same confidence all the women displayed during last night's lineup. Still, in my mind I could see girl after girl, counting her money: *Twenty, forty, sixty, eighty, one-hundred.*

Twenty, forty, sixty, eighty, two-hundred. Twenty, forty, sixty, eighty, three-hundred...

"What if I suck?"

This time, she tucked a piece of my own hair behind my ear. It was a gentle move. Protective. Almost motherly. "Then you go home. You don't do anything you're uncomfortable with. You can walk out anytime."

I looked up at her. "Would you get in trouble for that? If I walked out?"

Liberty shook her head. "No, silly. You might be young, but you're still an adult. I might get a little shit for bringing you in, but I've been here more than ten years. They're not going to bother me much."

I didn't know if I'd have the courage to stand—let alone dance—naked on a stage or solicit a dance from a man. I didn't know if this were the right choice, but somehow, on some level, the idea of trying felt exhilarating. Stripping was ridiculous to even consider, and yet, here I was, sitting in the Market Street Cinema, mulling it over.

"Alright then," I said. "I'll come back and work Monday dayshift with you."

CHAPTER EIGHT

I didn't recognize the person staring back at me in the mirror. I mean, she resembled me—a version of myself that I'd only expect from an airbrushed photo—but I just couldn't see *me*. Under the false lashes, glittered powder, and glossy lips, Lita had vanished. I turned to the side.

There's an ass I didn't have before.

The platform boots elongated my body, slimming my stomach, but also revealing a mysterious new roundness to my derriere. A flattering pair of boy shorts, the back hem just high enough to expose a perky set of cheeks, accented my newfound curvaceousness.

Liberty playfully snapped the strap on my top. "Are you sure this thing will be easy to take off?"

I ran a hand down the front, pulling it gently away from my stomach. "It looks like a corset, but it's just a soft top. It pulls over my head."

Standing next to each other, we contrasted like night and day. I wore nearly all black, and she stood in vibrant white. Her platinum coif eclipsed my loose, dark curls by nearly a full head. I was definitely the Midge to her Barbie, but that was fine by me.

Liberty began to walk toward the stairs. "Let's go check-in with Zakir."

With all the grace of a newborn calf taking its first steps, I followed in my towering boots.

Dancers entered to the side of Zakir's podium by way of a chute. It was narrow and tight, with room for no more than five girls in a single file. After some light small talk with Zakir, Liberty shuffled to the side to allow me forward.

"You dancing today, Lita?" His grin revealed a full set of white-veneered teeth. Apparently, cashier DJ's at strip clubs made good money.

I nodded.

Despite the grin, he didn't have the creep factor I expected. Instead, kindness lit his eyes, betraying the beefcake burliness of his frame. "Lolita, then."

Maybe he thought that was my full name. "Oh, no, just Lita."

"Lolita," he repeated, matter of factly. "No real names here, for safety. You're young so Lolita is good."

I understood the vague link between the name and some piece of literature I'd never read. *Lolita it is, then.*

"Take the stage at four." He scribbled against his clipboard.

I took this as a dismissal and moved out of the chute.

"You're lucky he's only having you dance once," Liberty said, after we passed beyond the podium. "Most girls, including me, have to dance twice."

I didn't feel terribly lucky. "I don't know how to dance at all."

She clucked her tongue. "Don't worry, babe. It's not even dancing. Just walk and roll around slowly. Take one thing off per song."

That didn't sound so hard. Except for taking things off. "I thought you said it was fifteen minutes?"

"It is, nearly. Three songs. First song, leave everything on. Second, take off your top. Third, take off your bottoms." She put her hand on the door pull. "You

73

don't dance for five hours, so there's time to see what happens."

She yanked the heavy door open. Barely eleven a.m., the floor was empty, except for two other girls chatting on the far end. "Most girls don't like to work Monday dayshift, but I think it's the best."

From where I was standing, I wasn't sure how that could be true. "How do you make any money in an empty club?"

"It's only empty now because the stage shows don't start until eleven-thirty."

"I still don't understand how that makes Monday dayshift the best," I replied.

Liberty giggled. "Most girls want to work nightshift, because it's packed—"

"Packed?" I scoffed. "I was here Friday, and there were only twenty guys, maybe."

Liberty shook her blond head. "You were only on the floor for the lineup. From ten until nearly two in the morning, it's a circus."

I still didn't understand. "But Monday dayshift is the best?"

"The Friday and Saturday night girls will be too tired to come in daytime Monday, plus they think it's dead.

But dayshift on a Monday has the best class of men. They've spent the weekend with their families, and most come during lunch in their suits. They have money and are here to spend it. Friday, Saturday? Those guys are just here to watch. Young guys in packs."

That made more sense but didn't answer everything. I shifted from one leg to the other. The boots were surprisingly comfortable.

Liberty put her hand on my shoulder and leaned in. "The dayshift girls are the ones who can't compete with the nightshift." She looked around, cautiously. "A smart dancer can clean up on a Monday. There's not the same level of competition."

I tried to zoom in on the chatting girls along the wall. I hadn't noticed before that both were in their forties and a little saggy around the middle. They looked good for their age, but I could see they wouldn't stand a chance next to Liberty. "Then why do they bother?"

"They do more. Other things. But you don't worry about that. It's not your problem."

More? "Liberty—?"

The music shot through the speakers in a blast. There was no question that Zakir loved his disco.

"Follow me!" Liberty shouted.

We walked to the padded wall I'd spotted—and kept clear of—last Friday. I reached out and pressed it, the floor-to-ceiling black pleather giving little resistance to my fingertips.

Liberty propped back against the padding. "This is for a wall dance. They are twenty dollars per song, same as lap dances in the audience. Forty if they are topless. This is the only place on the floor you can do topless dances." She began slowly sliding her backside up and down the wall, arching her chest forward. "If the wall is a man, I press back against him. Rub slowly."

I marveled at the silkiness of her movement. There was no embarrassment, and it looked surprisingly easy…for someone with the confidence to play sexy. "Do they…touch?"

"They touch." She cupped each of her breasts gently in her hands and began to massage them. "You can tell them not to, but I let them. I don't care."

I'd never considered myself a prude, but something felt really off about letting a stranger squeeze my boobs while I dry-humped him—all for the sticker price of twenty or forty dollars. Then, I remembered there was more. "What about private nude dances?"

In the same way she had clicked her stripper persona on and off the last time I'd seen her act, Liberty snapped out of seductive mode in a heartbeat. "Those are in the back!" She almost bounced off the wall.

I followed toward a pair of doors that looked like an emergency exit. Once through, a small table and a cash box sat manned by a friendly male attendant with an asymmetrical haircut.

"It's fifteen dollars for guys to come back here," Liberty said. The music was less intense but still vibrated the walls. "There's three areas. The first is full of curtained-off tables," she pointed as we walked past. Everything was padded in the black pleather, from tabletops to chairs.

She turned into the second entry, where we were met by the sound of a woman having an orgasm. A huge screen projected porn in a small, twenty-odd seat movie theater. Behind the seats was another padded wall for standing dances. "This is where men come to jack themselves off while watching porn or get a wall dance and let us do it with a grind. It's not as bad as it sounds."

"It's not as bad—?"

She was already out of the room before I finished my question. I chased her into the final room, which had

77

curtained-off areas with chairs instead of tables. In the back, there was a shower enclosed within a clear box. "What the f—?"

"Nobody uses that," Liberty interrupted. "If a guy wants to watch you shower you can offer it, but in all the time I've been here, I've never seen it used." She brushed past me back into the hallway.

I pointed to a locked door. "What's that for?"

"Mark hires a feature to come every week. They are usually porn stars, and they dance four main shows: two during dayshift and two at night. After, they do private dances in their room."

I quietly took it all in.

"Some girls say they charge a hundred dollars for fully nude, but most only charge eighty. Again, it's for however long you think is fair but usually one song. Two songs max."

"And touching back here?" I was afraid of what her answer might be. I could handle some boob groping, but I wasn't sure I could do more.

"There are girls here who do everything. *Everything.* But I don't allow hands between my legs. Tits and ass, fine. Nothing else." She spoke so casually about the sex trade that she might as well have been teaching me

78

to slice cookie dough. "You have to decide what's comfortable for you."

In a matter of a few weeks, I had gone from being a moderately shy college student to trying to determine how much of my body I was going to allow strange men to access. My inhibitions were being peeled away a layer at a time, but at a speed so fast it boggled my mind. I didn't know what I was going to be comfortable with, or if I was going to be comfortable with anything at all. But if I kept working ridiculous hours at Mod to scrape by, there was no way I would ever figure out what I actually wanted from life. It definitely wasn't this, but in the short term, if I was able to make some real money, the Cinema could provide enough quick cash to allow me to breathe a little.

It was a no-brainer for me. "I'm ready when you are, Liberty."

It took all of an hour to score my first client, and it was disgusting as hell. After being turned down by the only four men in the club, I pulled an older Chinese man who took no time at all to convince.

I sat on his lap, leaning in the way Liberty had with me. "Would you like a dance?" My voice had dropped to the best version of sultry I could muster. I felt absurd, not the least bit sexy.

His fingers looked like the knotted roots of a tree. I watched them rest on my thigh, nearly leaping out of his lap when he squeezed brusquely. "Very tight skin," he mumbled, more to himself than to me. His breath smelled like soured milk.

I stayed still, not sure how to respond to an answer that wasn't a no, but wasn't a yes either. My mind raced for something provocative to say. "Do you want to see the rest of me?"

Oh, I'm pretty damn good at this.

He nodded a simple yes and immediately followed me to the back rooms, paying his entry fee. I took him to a curtained-off booth with a chair.

I leaned back against the wall as he sat down. The nerve I'd just rallied disappeared, and I was again out of things to say. So I stuck to the basics. "It's forty for topless, eighty for fully nude."

Without saying a word, he reached into his coat pocket and handed me four twenties.

War erupted within my stomach, a battle between bitterness and butterflies. I was satisfied to have cash in hand—but no man had seen me naked since I'd broken up with the ex, and before him, there had only been one other. Now I stood in front of a man older than my father, about to put it all on display.

I tucked the bills into my stiff new wristlet.

Fuck it.

I pulled the top over my head. It was warm in the darkened cubicle, but my nipples still hardened. My fingers pressed downward toward my hips, sliding the boyshorts over my knees, down to my ankles. I stepped out of them and stood upright, exposing the full length of my body to my patron. He relaxed back in the chair, licking his lips. As soon as I lowered myself into a sitting position on his lap, I could feel his erection pressing into my thigh. The fabric of his Dockers felt rough against my bare bottom.

He grasped my breast and began to massage. I couldn't help but stare down at his wrinkled hand as he squeezed away on my tit. "Call me Daddy."

My body stiffened with sudden shyness. He either didn't notice or didn't care and continued kneading my flesh with his leathery fingers. I too could pretend I either didn't notice or didn't care and ignored the request.

For two songs, I rocked in a gentle hover over his lap while his hands freely roamed the length of my body, plying and pinching steadily. He made two attempts to probe between my legs, but after playfully swatting his hands away both times, he didn't try again. I rewarded him by giving him what he asked for instead, having grown bolder with each second that passed. "Am I being a good girl, Daddy?"

This clearly excited him, and his putrid breath became more pronounced as his breathing quickened.

My Chinese daddy paid well. I accepted one twenty-dollar bill after another as the seconds turned into minutes. My disgust began to dissipate, and the distastefulness of it all became sadly tolerable. By the time I pulled the curtain aside and left the enclave in my dance garb, I had taken enough money off one customer to pay half a month's rent.

And it only cost me every last shred of dignity I possessed.

CHAPTER NINE

"**C**an I get the chicken fajitas and a side of guacamole?"

The cashier nodded without a smile and punched the order into his cash register. "Fourteen dollars." It sounded like he said *fart-teen* with his Scottish brogue.

"Lita!"

I spun around and stood face to face with my mother. The shock must have registered. She opened her arms and pulled me into them. "I didn't mean to scare you, honey!"

I'd always loved the sweet smell of her gardenia perfume, but today it made me feel a bit sick.

"Fourteen dollars," the uncheerful Scot repeated impatiently.

"Oh, let me get that." Mom reached into her heavy purse. "Add another of whatever she's having too. I've worked up an appetite, having to hunt my own daughter down. Are you sure you don't want anything else, Lita?"

I only wanted to leave. "I'm good. Thanks, Mom."

She retrieved her credit card with a smooth, elegant hand. Her fingernails were painted in their signature color, Flashbulb Fuchsia, which popped against her golden tan. "You sure? It's on me."

I was immediately ashamed. The only thing I hated more than my parents thinking I was broke was the idea of them knowing why I wasn't. I gave the best smile I could manage. "I'm fine, Mom. Really."

It was the truth, even if it was uncomfortable. After I had paid the house fee and tipped out Zakir— giving him enough so I didn't have to dance on stage—I'd made the same as I would've working a full week at Mod. Beginners luck, Liberty called it. It didn't feel lucky.

The cashier handed us a laminated number to place on the side of whichever table we chose and a stack of far more napkins than we could possibly use.

"What are you doing here, Mom?"

The cashier leaned forward over the counter. "You need to find a place to sit so you don't hold up the line." His voice rose from slight annoyance to downright frustration as it rumbled through the restaurant. The empty restaurant, as it was, with no line to hold up.

Mom crinkled her nose and chuckled gently. "I think we'd better find a seat."

We picked a table by the window, and she motioned me into a seat with a view toward the mall's parking lot. I stared out, watching people go about their day-to-day lives. Normal people with normal jobs. Not like me.

"Penny for your thoughts?" Mom asked, teasingly.

My face burned. "I'm sorry, Mom. I'm just trying to find my bearings, you know."

She put up her hand to stop me. "I wouldn't know, since I can't seem to ever get ahold of you." Her eyes narrowed. "You must have a home phone by now."

There was no good reason to lie to her about that. "Remind me to give it to you before we leave."

Mom's hair had regrown in a soft chestnut brown, lighter after the chemotherapy, and she kept her curls cropped neatly. They bobbed slightly as she shook her head and laughed. "Oh no! You're giving it to me now!" She took a pen from her purse and handed it to me. "Write it down on one of those napkins. Lord knows we have enough of them."

I accepted the pen and scribbled down my new phone number. Mom grabbed the napkin the moment I stopped writing. "I'm tired of staking out an ambush at your underwear store. You know I don't like going in there."

Neither she nor my father were happy when they learned of the job at Mod. Of course, to some degree, that was part of why I wanted to work there.

A woman brought our food to the table and set it down carefully. I was grateful for the distraction.

Mom didn't let the calm last long. "How come you haven't called?"

I pushed a piece of sizzling chicken around the plate with my fork. I didn't know how to respond, except to redirect the focus back onto her. "You and Dad told me to leave, Mom. How do you expect me to live on my own without working a thousand hours a week?"

Mom's mouth was full of food, and she put her finger to her lips, frowning and swallowing hastily. "That's totally unfair, Lita. We didn't tell you to leave, we told you to go to college. You decided to leave instead. You think that was what we hoped you'd choose?"

"I don't think most parents make their kids choose at all, Mom."

Her eyes went sad. "I don't have the energy to fight with you or your father. There's been too much of that."

My heart sunk at this confession. I didn't want my parents squabbling on account of me, even if I thought their ultimatum was heavy-handed. It wasn't easy, but overall I was enjoying my freedom, even if I, quite literally, had to work my ass off to fund it. "I don't want to fight either. Let's not talk about it."

I wanted nothing more than for this conversation to be over. Parts of my life now were off limits, and the less we broached those parts, the less I would be forced to lie about them.

"Good," she replied, matter-of-factly, "but I still want to help you."

This didn't sound like *let's not talk about it.* I continued to eat.

"Let me help you, Lita."

I scooped a chunk of chicken into a tortilla and globbed a spoonful of sour cream into it. "I don't need help, but thank you."

Mom's hand disappeared under the table, and when it came back up she was holding a checkbook.

"Mom—"

"Lita, please. This is so awful! I don't know how you are going to be able to manage all the expense of living on your own working in retail." Her voice was trembling, almost panicked. "And even if you can make ends meet, you won't have time for anything else. I don't want that life for my girl."

My mind tumbled in a whirlwind, a tornado of emotional overload. "Mom, seriously, don't—"

"It doesn't matter," she replied, straightening her back again. She folded back the face of the checkbook and started writing. "Just take this. It'll be our secret."

"I won't take it, Mom. Believe me when I say I don't want your money." I meant it sincerely, even if my heart constricted at the reason why.

She looked confused. "If you say you don't want it, that's fine. But *need* is different than *want*. I know what you have saved and what you make. How can you say you don't need it?"

I was again at a loss as for words, especially since I didn't have a clear-cut answer. "I've picked up extra shifts, and my rent is shockingly low for the area. Also, I think I've found a part-time job." I plucked up a cube of chargrilled chicken and popped it in my mouth before it revealed more.

"Where?"

"Nowhere exciting, but it will help me out. Let me do this myself, Mom. I have to at least try." I couldn't hide the hint of resignation in my voice.

She reached her hand across the table and took my fist, which I hadn't realized was clenched, into her own. "It's okay, Lita. I know you can do it. I just want to lighten your load."

"You buy lunch when we go out. That's enough."

She squeezed my hand and laughed before releasing it. "At least let me give you a little something to buy some chocolate chips. I sure do miss your cookies!"

Her laugh was infectious, and my heavy heart lifted a little. "I'll always have cookies for you, Mom."

"That's my baby."

It was hard to feel anything but love for my mom, however pushy she could be. Through two lengthy battles with breast cancer, she carried on smiling. She gave what she could to anyone she could. She was a generous, loving woman. Embarrassingly naive sometimes, but a purer heart than hers, I had yet to find. Yet as badly as she wanted to help, I had to do this myself.

"I have to get back to work in ten minutes. My lunch break is almost over."

"Pot roast was always one of your favorites. Why don't you bake some cookies for dessert and come home for dinner Monday?"

The last thing I wanted to do was turn her down, but I had to work all week, and I planned to go back to the Cinema on Monday. Between the two jobs, I would be working six days a week. The less I explained to my parents, especially when overly exhausted, the better. "I can't this week, but I'll keep you posted."

We stood and I leaned in, giving Mom a tight hug. I made my exit quickly, disappearing through the door and walking through the mall until I knew I was out of view. Instead of going back to Mod, I scurried into the public bathroom and locked myself in a stall, spending the last minutes of my break sobbing over the toilet.

I could handle doing dark deeds in a San Francisco gentleman's club, but lying to the people I loved would destroy me.

CHAPTER TEN

At least half the girls who showed up to dance were drunk within the first forty-five minutes of signing in. Generally, those were also the same girls who sold much more of their bodies for far less money, although it wasn't as prevalent during dayshift. Hand jobs were a different story, and I think there were probably less than ten of us that didn't offer them. However, I was beginning to understand why Liberty said, if you were smart, you could make money. Truly though, smarts had less to do with it; the key was to be sober…and most women had a difficult time working at the Cinema without the aid of liquid courage.

Going in, I had been convinced that the seediest part of stripping would be the actual stripping. That was pure guilelessness on my part. The seediest part of adult entertainment was the drugs, alcohol, and all the reasons behind why the girls were working there in the first place. Some were dropped off by men that Zakir barred from entry. Mark didn't allow pimps in the Cinema, no matter what they offered in bribes. Many an arm was covered in the frightening combination of bruises and track marks, and those girls usually worked everyday, sometimes double shifts to support their habits.

I'd seen two dancers with deep scarring over their wrists, one vertically, one horizontally. The vertical girl made no secret of her opinion that the other had only slit hers as a cry for help, while she had actually gone in whole hog. Liberty said they only got into arguments about it when they were high, but I never stuck around to find out. I spent as little time as possible in the dungeon dressing room. I was there to make money, not friends.

But that didn't stop the girls from approaching me anyway:

"I have a friend outside who will help you make hella extra money."

"Come back to the hotel with me after work. I want you to meet Tony."

"Do you know where I can buy some better shit? This shit is makin' me trip out."

Luckily, nobody really remembered what they said or offered by the following Monday.

Everyone at the Cinema had a story, and mine was the least interesting of them all: a privileged teenager refused to accept her parents' full-ride offer for college and instead ended up on Market Street? I went ahead and kept that gem to myself.

It was virtually the same motley crew every Monday, but I preferred that. Change made me uneasy, and a new face with a different swagger could eat into my confidence. And despite how all the women appeared the first time I saw them line up, confidence was actually in short supply here.

It took a supremely self-assured woman to offer her boobs up for forty dollars, only to be repeatedly rejected by men she wouldn't give the time of day to outside the club. Thus, everyone lied about how much she made. If you say you had a bad day and all you had to show for it was the house fee, it meant you spent hours peddling your body, but only a few patrons said yes. That was understandably humiliating but also understandably common.

I never talked about the job at all, except with Liberty. I understood why they made it sound like they had hustled a grand by clock-out at seven-thirty but not why they were talking about it in the first place. I wouldn't trust any of these women once I stepped outside the club. You start babbling about having a thousand dollars in your wristlet, and you're almost guaranteed to be robbed on your way to BART.

"You want to go out for dinner when we're done here?" Charleston spoke in a slow southern drawl. I spent half her sentences watching the clock, wondering when she was going to be finished.

"Thanks, Charlie, but I'm half-dead already."

She clucked her tongue. "Too bad. Basil and I were going to a new place in Concord. It's supposed to be good."

There was no chance I was going to spend an evening with Charleston and her grubby, grabby husband. The one time I'd spoken to him when he'd come to collect his wife, he went on and on about how he was writing a book about the keys to successful real estate investing. I asked if he was going to include having a wife who made a half-grand a day. He didn't think it was funny.

"Sorry, Charlie." I winked and distracted myself by soliciting a passing man.

He ignored me entirely.

Liberty waltzed up. "How's your day so far?" She pulled a tube of lipstick from her wristlet and began dabbing her puckered lips.

"I made quota but only have twenty over." I'd learned the lingo fast. Nobody said *house fee* on the floor. Saying *quota* was all the rage in the glitter mines. "You?"

"Nada," she replied, tucking the tube away safely.

I didn't expect to hear that. "It's nearly one o'clock. You haven't had a single dance?"

"Nope." She didn't sound concerned, but Liberty rarely sounded concerned about anything. "What was Miss Belle over there talking about?"

I laughed. "She was asking me out to dinner…with her husband."

Liberty extended her tongue and made a choking sound. There was nothing more that really needed to be said.

"Haven't any of your regulars come in today?"

She shook her head. "My regulars are starting to become a little less regular these days. I think they're finding themselves girls who will go the extra mile for them."

I was sad to hear that. Regulars were the one thing that kept most girls consistently earning, especially for someone like me who only worked a day a week. I would be happy with two or three good regulars, safe in the knowledge that I'd get a hundred from each of them every week. I could pick up the rest in one-off dances from casual customers. Liberty had several regulars, but they stretched over the five, sometimes six, days she worked each week. "I don't know why they'd want someone else."

She looked at me like I was a sweet, silly child. "To tickle their pickles, of course."

This time I stuck out my tongue and made a choking noise.

"They need to clean this place up, but Mark makes sure we don't have issues with the law. It hurts us all that girls can do anything here without trouble."

I had heard girls talk about how other clubs had strict enforcement against even touching, but somehow the Cinema and the Century skirted this. "How come you never worked at one of the other clubs?"

"I've worked at other clubs," she replied. "I've been here for a long time, but I worked at other places when I was younger."

This surprised me. I knew she'd been in the game for over a decade, but I didn't know it had been much longer. "Why did you leave if they were cleaner?"

She leaned her head back against the wall and sighed. "Look around, Lita. This isn't exactly the A-squad for dancers. Mark hires anyone. There's no auditions or try-outs. He knows it's a glorified brothel. I didn't leave the other clubs, I got too old to work them."

It wasn't the first time she'd brought up her age, nor was it the first time I'd tried to contradict her. But there was no point. "You were the one who said it was better to be the hottest girl on dayshift than a needle in a haystack on night, right? So here you are. The hot Monday girl."

Liberty tilted her head slightly and looked at me out of the corner of her eye. "I need to make a lot more money very fast, or I'll never get that tea shop."

"You'll get your shop." I believed it. And she certainly deserved it.

"That one's yours, isn't he?"

A shadow approached from the corner, and a hulking, six-foot-six ex-linebacker came into view. I would be making some real money for the day. "That's Ted. He was here last week too."

Liberty put her hand on my shoulder. "Go get 'em, Tiger."

He wore his dirty-blond hair combed in a side part but was constantly pushing it up off his forehead. At first I thought he was just lazy with his haircuts, until my breasts were pressed against his cheeks. From above I could see that he had a seriously receding hairline.

"Hey, Ted."

He smiled, exposing two front teeth that overlapped like crossed fingers. "Are you available?"

When I motioned my head to the back, he followed me like a huge, three-hundred-pound puppy. I yanked the curtain closed. "It's good to see you again."

He gave a sheepish grin, pulling his chair up. With his height, even seated, we were nearly eye to eye. "I couldn't stay away. I really like you."

It was nice to hear but hard to believe. He didn't know me. The last time, we'd exchanged only a handful of pleasantries before he spent the next forty-five minutes with his sweaty forehead pressed into my naked back, grinding his hard-on against my ass cheeks. "That's sweet of you to say."

He stared at me, seemingly expecting more.

"Um..." I tried to bumble on. "How have you been?"

"Good, good," he replied. "I got promoted at work. I can't complain about that."

Small talk got under my skin even in the most mundane of circumstances. To feign interest and exchange chitchat in a dingy cubicle made for lewd conduct? That was miles beyond my limited skill set. "I'm happy to hear that."

He rubbed his palms back and forth across the top of his jeans like a nervous child. Neither of us said anything, and for once I was grateful for the thumping music in the background. Finally, his expression changed to surprise, and he reached in his pocket, dragging out a wad of folded bills. "Oh, sorry!" He counted out one hundred-sixty dollars in twenties and handed them to me. "Just like last week?"

I took the notes and stuffed them in my wristlet, elated at the possibility of a new regular. The smile came naturally. "Just like last week, then." I removed my top and boyshorts, tossing them to the far end of the table. Being naked felt strangely commonplace now. Ridiculously, I felt comfortable nude but weirded out by conversation. I felt a little bad that I couldn't come up with some chitchat, but at the end of the day, this was a job and Ted was a customer.

I turned my back to him and bent forward, spreading my legs and leaning on my elbows across the table. He placed his hands on my hips, sliding them up and down over my thighs and lower back, then guided me gently onto his lap. The solid stiffness of his erection pressed into my bottom, which I began rotating in slow circular motions. Instead of pushing harder against me, he fell back slightly and readjusted his position on the chair.

It was the first time someone had retreated when I'd offered my ass, and I wasn't sure what to make of that.

"Just relax," he whispered, massaging my shoulders.

I had always carried a world of tension in my neck and shoulders, and I could feel it being released as he kneaded my muscles. I relaxed into him instinctively and allowed this man to give me pleasure—something I hadn't experienced for a long time. After a short while, I stopped counting songs, losing track of time while he moved his hands in slow, therapeutic strokes over my strained muscles.

I released a light moan.

It wasn't sexual, not for me at least, but it certainly was for him. I felt the press of his hard-on again, but this time I didn't move.

"That feels so good," I exhaled, not caring if he believed I meant his dick as opposed to the massage.

He continued firmly stroking my back but began rubbing himself against my ass. As the pressure in his jeans became more intense, the massage became slightly less rhythmic and a little deeper than I could handle. Knowing my turn was up, I leaned ahead and set my forearms on the table, raising my buttocks in the air and rolling forward until my chest and stomach rested flat on the table. Ted stood behind me, grinding his erection against my backside with an increased vigor that matched his breathing. His hands, the same ones that had only moments before been massaging me tenderly, now raced along the length of my body, grasping for flesh indiscriminately. In a silent, jerky movement that I knew signaled his climax, he made a final push and then collapsed back into his chair.

I reached behind to feel my own ass, testing for a wetness that I always prayed wouldn't be there. Most grinders were courteous enough to arrive wearing condoms—even on their limp dicks. It was more a precaution against leaving with a wet spot on their pants than any real care or concern for us, but nevertheless, we appreciated it. Ted clearly knew the drill.

Still catching his breath, he asked, "You're here every Monday?"

"I am," I replied, stepping into my bottoms. I gave him a full smile. "Will you be here every Monday?"

"Now that I got my promotion, I hope so. I live in Lafayette, so, not far from Frisco."

I quickly finger-combed through my hair and smoothed it down, then straightened my top. "Good. Where are you from originally?"

His forehead crinkled and his eyes narrowed. "I moved here from Los Angeles three years ago. How did you know I'm not from the Bay Area?"

"Because nobody calls it Frisco except tourists."

He gave me a cheesy smile and a thumbs-up as I reopened the curtain, stepping out into the common area. "Have a great week," I tossed over my shoulder.

That was all the small talk I could handle.

CHAPTER
ELEVEN

Monday nights were sacrosanct. I could not and would not be bothered. I had a schedule and had become moderately obsessive about adhering to it, a strange attribute for someone who was so disorganized in every other aspect of her life. Still, a lonely schedule was relatively easy to stick to when you had no friends, no boyfriend, and were avoiding your family like the plague.

I worked at Mod Tuesday through Saturday. Usually I'd come in halfway through Amelia's morning shift and be off halfway through Sandra's closing shift. I enjoyed working with both of them and counted it as points toward a social life.

Sunday was my only full day off, and I spent in with a wonderfully late sleep-in and then an afternoon of baking. The bulk of my confections would make their way up to Patty, who was always grateful to receive them.

"My diet can wait until the next Tuesday after never!" she would always say with a giggle.

Sunday nights, between midnight and one in the morning, I'd do my grocery shopping. Safeway was open twenty-four hours, and I had quickly learned that my dollar would spread the furthest by shopping during vampire hours. Most households did their major shopping during the day Sunday, but Sunday night, when everyone was supposed to be in bed, that was when the meat got marked down to less than half price. Even though I was making enough to live comfortably, I was saving every penny I could, still more or less living within the budget I'd created when I thought I'd only be working retail.

When Monday rolled around, I worked eleven a.m. until seven p.m. at the Cinema, but Monday nights, when I got home, that was when I settled in and enjoyed the fruits of my labor. I ordered a pizza, which felt like an absolute luxury after an exhausting day, and showered while waiting for it to be delivered. With my hair combed into a wet ponytail and my freshly scrubbed body wrapped in a faded flannel nightshirt, I hunkered down on the sofa with my little slices of heaven and watched my favorite TV lineup. It started at nine with Ally McBeal and ended just before midnight after two episodes of Bob and Margaret. These were my Monday night staples, and I was married to them.

Done with the pizza but only halfway through Dr. Katz, the phone rang. I knew who it was. Her half-dozen messages on the answering machine were all the same:

"Lita? Lita, honey...? Are you there?"

The dejection in her voice came through as clearly as her words. It made my heart ache.

"Lita, if you're there...please answer the phone."

Dad mumbled something in the background.

"She's not picking up," Mom whispered.

He mumbled again.

"I called there. They said Sunday and Monday were her off days."

My body jolted upright; Amelia or Sandra had told them my schedule!

The conversation continued between them, with Dad murmuring and Mom responding in hushed whispers, until the machine cut them off.

Going *no contact* with my mother was proving difficult. It was agonizing for me. Not only was she desperately persistent but also I wanted to talk to her. It was torture for her because she was convinced I was angry, or overworked, or struggling—or all three. I missed her and my father, but it was easier to dodge their calls than to blatantly lie to them.

Maybe I was also afraid that I might cave in.

At nineteen, I lived like a seventy-year old spinster. Well, except for the part where I was a stripper. But I didn't care. I'd had my heart broken and my life turned upside down. I didn't know where I was headed or what I wanted to do, but finally, I felt independent, as happy as I'd ever been. Sure, I would have preferred to be able to make the same money that I did with my clothes on, but I couldn't…and so I just cracked on and did what I needed to do.

The phone rang again.

Hi, sorry I'm not here to take your call. Leave a message at the beep.

"Lita, honey, call me when you get home. I won't be able to sleep until you do."

106

I had moved out, but they were still asking me to wake them up when I got home. The phone cord, it appeared, also doubled as an umbilical cord.

"We haven't heard from you in ages, honey. We're starting to worry."

Dad mumbled.

"I might go to her underwear store tomorrow," Mom replied to him.

I raced to the kitchen pulled the phone from its cradle. "I'm here, Mom."

"Oh, thank God! She picked up!"

I had answered the phone but remained a third party to their conversation. "Mom?"

"Yes, yes Lita! Where have you been?"

I looped the coils of the cord around my index finger. "I told you I might be getting a second job." That was true.

"She said she got another job…"

More garbled jibberish from Dad.

I wasn't in the right frame of mind to go through this with them but needed to appease her to keep her from going into Mod. I'd rather lie over the phone than to her face. "Mom?"

"I'm sorry, honey. I was just telling your dad you got another job."

"I know. I can hear you."

"Where are you wor—?"

"Mom, I'm really tired and I need to rest. I just wanted you to know that I'm fine. I'm working a lot." That was also true.

She cleared her throat. "I still have that thing from lunch that I think you should take, honey."

Nice try, Mom, but I still can't take your check. "Thanks but no thanks. I really need to go. I love you."

I hung up before she could ask when we could meet up again, clicking the ringer into silent mode. My favorite night of the week couldn't be interrupted again, although having verified that I was at home and safe, it was unlikely she'd call back again tonight.

I opened the refrigerator, then scanned its contents. A bowl with half a batch of cookie dough remained right where I'd left it the day before. I needed to work on portioning, since my convection oven couldn't bake up a full batch. As I spooned the dough into a neat row, I remembered the promise I'd made to bring some to my mother. I needed a stronger story so I could stop avoiding her and rebuild my relationship with both parents.

A stronger story or, better yet, an actual plan for my life.

I clicked the oven on.

It took my parents kicking me out to find myself, even if the path I'd found remained unclear: College was off the table. I didn't want a career at Mod. Stripping was just a quick means to get by and pad my savings account.

A stronger story at this point would probably be easier. . . but a plan would be better. I wanted more for myself. I wanted a clear path.

When will I have a plan?

Patty's voice rattled in my head. "Next Tuesday after never!"

CHAPTER
TWELVE

Dancing on stage was a waste of time and energy, at least on dayshift. I usually tipped Zakir out an extra twenty so I wouldn't have to, but today there weren't enough girls so I didn't have a choice. Some dancers relished it, but I wasn't one of them. Aside from not wanting to be on display, the only money was in lap dances. The most I'd ever made on stage was a whopping seven dollars, and even the most creative dancers didn't do better than that.

The exception to this were the features, highly promoted and quasi-famous adult entertainers. Currently, the feature was a South Korean porn star named Mi-sook, who billed herself as the largest-breasted Asian in the world. If a man placed a five-dollar bill on the stage, she'd roll it up like a cigarette, put it in his mouth, and let him slide it into her cooter with his teeth. She always had a line of men outside her private room after the shows.

I was no Mi-sook, with her 54KKK cups and provocative stage tricks. Almost entirely by accident, I had learned two pole tricks, but that was hardly remarkable. Pole tricks only looked difficult; they were shockingly easy. Even before I'd figured out how to grip and spin, I was able to build a whole little show around a few walking turns and slides. The men didn't care about acrobatics; they were there to see my *cunny*. Jiggle my boobs, open my legs, rinse and repeat. I threw in the stunts just to entertain myself.

I closed my set of three songs and put my outfit back on. I didn't even bother changing into a costume. I looked good in my standard corset, boy-shorts, and boots, and I knew better than to mess with a good thing.

Waiting down the stretch was a regular of mine. A Sikh in his late forties, he told me his name was Lahkwinder, but he went by the nickname of Lucky. Lucky for me, he had shown up. Or maybe not. Lucky pushed the limits of what I found acceptable.

"Why were you up there today?" He twisted the hem of his shirt back and forth.

"We're short girls. Do you want to go in the back?" Fewer girls meant more opportunity to make money. I wasn't about to waste time with small talk.

He bobbed his head and followed me back to a curtained-off table.

"The usual," Lucky stated. A small business owner, he'd displayed an impressive level of business acumen last time by negotiating a flat rate with me. When I nodded, he handed me two-hundred and eighty dollars. With a grunt, he sat down, pulling his chair to the edge of the padded table.

"Facing forward or toward the wall?" Forward meant I'd have to look at him, but toward the wall required a level of trust we hadn't quite established yet, so I preferred forward.

"Forward first."

I slid the straps of my top down my arms, exposing my breasts. The fabric clung to my stomach just how he liked it. I leaned back onto the table, hoisting myself up gently.

"Can I?" His voice had dropped into a rasp.

I reclined back, onto my elbows, and lightly elevated my hips "You can."

He let out a gravelly moan, extending his fingers forward and slithering them up the outside of my thighs. His fingertips hooked over the top of my boy shorts, pulling them to my ankles. I lifted one boot and tugged it through the leg of the pantie, leaving the other side dangling. Lucky had a thing for panties on the ankle.

My knees butterflied to each side, presenting my most intimate hollow to the man in the chair.

The crinkle of a condom wrapper was barely noticeable above the throb of music. The first time I'd heard it, I panicked. But not anymore.

Lucky stood up, his eyes planted between my thighs as he slipped the condom down a meager shaft. Its size was further diminished by an overgrown bush that looked like it was swallowing the poor thing whole.

He sat back down and started stroking himself slowly.

The first couple of times he'd brought me back for this, I kept nervously watching to make sure I wasn't going to get pounced. I made sure I always knew where his hands were and that his little pecker didn't try to make a move. Now I was relaxed. Bored, even. Occasionally

Lucky would move his face so it was under a foot from my slit—but all he wanted was a sniff. He'd inhale deeply, then release a controlled, steamy exhale. The whole time, he serviced himself.

And I waited.

And waited.

And waited.

He huffed and puffed, jerking his arm until it accelerated into frantic pumping. Except for his erratic breathing, he remained mostly silent until he discharged a low groan and snort combination with his climax.

Today he had only taken forty-five minutes, but the deal was that I stayed put until he finished. So far this was the longest he'd taken.

I tugged my straps and panties back up, crossing my legs and smoothing the back of my hair. "It was good to see you again, Lucky."

He finished swabbing his penis with a box of tissues the Cinema kept conveniently in each curtained-off room. "I want to see you again next week but not here." Lucky zipped his trousers.

I had no interest in seeing anyone outside the club. Punch in, punch out, go home. "I don't date, Lucky."

He took a fresh tissue and wiped his hands. "I don't want a date. I want to do this at my place."

I knew I was officially a seasoned sex worker when I started using the lingo. "By date I meant doing what we do now, not a relationship. It's a date when it's outside the club, even if you pay for it." It also meant I would no longer be just a dancer but an escort. "I don't work outside of the Cinema."

He tossed the crumpled tissue paper toward a black basket in the corner but missed. "You haven't even asked me how much I'd pay you."

I crossed my hands over my chest. "It wouldn't matter." That wasn't entirely true. Everyone had a price, even me.

"I have a store in Sebastopol. Do you know where that is?"

I had spent some magical summer days running around the apple orchards in the area. My great-aunt had lived and died in tiny little Sebastopol. It surprised me that Lucky lived there, not least because it was a decent hour-and-a-half drive from San Francisco. "Sonoma County, right? I know where it is."

"Meet me next Monday at the store. Take the day off, and I'll pay you for your day."

It was a tempting offer, spending a day in the California wine country while still making what I would in the club...but it wasn't safe. I knew all the Cinema offered was a false sense of security, but I was familiar with its dark corners. Even though I was aware of the risk those corners might hold, the customers who came in weren't. There were no surveillance cameras, but the presumption that there were kept the men in check. A store, even in idyllic Sebastopol, wouldn't offer that protection. "I can't, Lucky. I'm sorry."

He reached in his pocket and pulled out a card. "Call me if you change your mind."

I plucked it from his hand and tucked it into my wristlet. "I don't—"

He was on the other side of the curtain before I could tell him that I wouldn't be changing my mind.

Many girls here dreamed of escort work. It was easy to imagine a rich man riding in and offering you the world, even if the world meant having your rent paid and getting enough spending money to be a one-customer kind of woman. It wasn't as easy to imagine a normal guy with a convenience store in the 'burbs walking in and offering you a day off from hustling.

"Lolita to the front." Zakir's voice blazed through the building's sound system like the voice of God.

What could he want?

I'd never been called to the front before. It better not mean he wanted me to do another stage show.

I walked quickly through the floor, pushing through the heavy theater doors and entering the chute. Zakir didn't look up from the stack of CD's he was sorting. "Your guy Ted called. Said he won't be in today."

It would have been a killer day if Ted had made it. After Lucky, my Chinese daddy, and a handful of small lap dances, Ted's cash would have made for my best day yet. "Thanks, Zakir."

He smirked, still sifting. "You have him wrapped around your finger, no?"

"I wouldn't say it's my finger he's wrapped around."

Finally Zakir looked up. "Atta girl, Lolita."

I was getting used to the name, but that didn't mean I liked it. I winked and turned to go.

"How much to get in?" The voice sent a chill down my spine, and I forced my back flush against the wall, dragging myself out of sight. I knew that voice.

"Fifteen for the front, another fifteen for the back." Zakir looked to me and raised an eyebrow.

I pointed my finger toward the front of the podium and silently mouthed, *I know him.*

He held up his hand in acknowledgment. "Not too many girls working today. Maybe you come back after the shift change in a couple hours."

"I don't have time to wait a couple hours."

Zakir took a city map and pen from a drawer. "Our other club, New Century, is here." He marked the map. "There's the Regal just down here, which is a peep show. Girls behind glass." He continued scribbling. "Here's Deja Vu, and Mitchell Brothers is right there."

I heard the paper being picked up. "Thanks, man. I'll check them out."

Zakir kept looking straight ahead until the man left, then turned to me. "We can't turn business away, Lolita."

I was too terrified to think about anything but getting out of there. I slapped a twenty on the counter. "I know. Thanks, Zakir."

The twenty was picked up and stuffed into the pocket of his jeans. "That helps."

119

"I can't be here if he comes back. I paid the quota before noon. Can I go home now?"

He flicked his hand. "Go."

I flew down those precipitous steps without any fear of hurtling to my death. In all of five minutes, I'd thrown on my street clothes and cleared out my locker.

As I raced out the front door, Zakir's voice trailed after me, "Lolita, who was that, anyway?"

"Mr. Hunter." His name left a tannic taste in my mouth, like a dirty penny. "My favorite high school science teacher."

CHAPTER
THIRTEEN

Liberty stretched her legs out on the sofa and put a plate of ginger-spiced snickerdoodles on her lap. "These might be the best things I've ever tasted."

After a restless night, I'd called her in a panic. She calmed me down, suggested I play sick at Mod for a couple days, and came straight over. It was the first time someone besides my mother had dropped everything to be with me. All the cookies in the world couldn't hold a candle to that kind of sweetness. "Have some more."

She picked another up and took a bite. "These would be great with a strong, dark tea."

"A tea pairing? Like what people do with wine?" My parents enjoyed wine pairings, but I couldn't stand the stuff. I wasn't old enough to buy it anyway.

"Mmm," she replied, chewing slowly. "Exactly like that. The smoky, nutty flavor of Lapsang Souchong would offset the spice in these."

"Maybe I'll try that sometime." *If I can find the time.* "My work schedule is crazy. I don't know when I'd be able to hunt down a fancy tea."

"I get mine from a few different shops in Chinatown, but my little boutique will have plenty of teas from all over the place. Oh, a Summer Flush Darjeeling would be great with these too."

I admired Liberty's enthusiasm. I wish I had that kind of passion for something and an outlet to pursue it. "How did you learn so much about tea?"

There was a clink as she set the plate of snickerdoodles on the glass coffee table. "A little bit of reading, a couple classes, and a whole lot of drinking. I've tried just about everything." She rubbed her hands together. "That reminds me. I have some exciting news!"

I settled into the loveseat adjacent to her. "More exciting than discovering a favorite teacher is a lecher?" Discovering that Mr. Hunter paid to see naked women was disturbing. I couldn't image him in one of the dark rooms, a topless stripper grinding on him, but that still wasn't what had really been bothering me. He, or anyone else, could walk into the Cinema at anytime to find me working there, and that put my anxiety into overdrive. I was terrified of being seen there.

Liberty laughed. "That's not exciting, that's interesting. And don't worry about things like that. Remember, it would be more embarrassing for him than it would be for you."

I wasn't so sure, but right in this moment, that didn't matter. "Sorry, Liberty, I was being selfish. What's your exciting news?"

She let out an excited squeak, making it hard to remember that she had twenty-five years on me. "I'm going to Japan!"

I shot up, ramrod straight. "What? When? Wait, why?" The spitfire questions came out in a ramble. Japan sounded exciting but also totally random.

"I know some girls who have gone to Tokyo to dance, and they made tons of money. A fortune." She wagged a finger. "But that's only part of the reason."

Here I had been concerned about the safety of driving to Sonoma County for a private dance, and Liberty was thinking of jet-setting off to another country. She was smart enough to know what she was doing, even if I wasn't going to be able to understand it. I was still skeptical. "What's the real reason for going?"

"Kyoto is a three hour train ride from Tokyo. I'm going to dance in Tokyo on the weekends and learn the art of Japanese tea service in Kyoto during the week!" Another squeal escaped her lips. "Isn't that just the best?"

I picked up the plate of cookies and brought them to the kitchen, more out of shock than necessity. "How long will you be gone?" My voice didn't relay the degree of excitement that absolutely dripped from hers.

She snickered. "Don't worry, kitten. I'll only be there for six weeks. Though, if the money's good, I will probably go again for longer."

I felt bad about not being happier for her. "The tea course takes longer than six weeks?"

"Oooooph!" She rubbed her temples with her fingertips. "It takes a solid year to master the Japanese tea service, but I'll learn the basics. I'd go back to work because I really, really need to make as much as possible with the little time I have left to dance. There's a shelf life to this, you know."

Her plan was solid. A couple of women well into their fifties still worked at the Cinema, but I knew they offered more than Liberty did. I was mostly sad about my only friend moving over five-thousand miles away. "I'll miss you." It came out in a sigh.

Liberty stood and came to me, wrapping her arms around my shoulders. "You need to make as much as you can as quickly as you can and get out." She squeezed tighter. "Don't be doing this in your forties with nothing to show for it. . . like me."

"This isn't all for nothing with you, Liberty. You're working toward something. I'm just working."

"You have time on your side," she replied. "But you can't waste it." She let me go, leaning her back against the refrigerator and crossing her arms. "Tell me about the offer you got from your Punjabi guy."

Lucky. His card had moved from my wristlet to the garbage can. "He offered to buy out my day if I drove to Sebastopol for a private dance."

"Did he specify how much exactly that would be?"

I shook my head. "He's a shrewd negotiator. I don't think it'll be as good as it sounds."

She looked up at the speckled drywall ceiling, pursing her lips. "You're making about four-hundred a day, on average?"

"Closer to five-fifty." This week had been even better, but we were talking averages.

Her stare remained fixed on my ceiling. "Good God, Lita. That's a shit-ton of cash for a Monday dayshift."

"I've seen Charleston count out more, and some of the other girls talk about making over seven-hundred." I didn't know why I felt so defensive.

"Charlie does hand-jobs, and the other girls are liars." She leveled her eyes with mine. "I might make what you do on a nightshift, but I've also paid the quota out-of-pocket twice in the last month."

My heart sank. The thought of Liberty paying to work at the Cinema was enough to make me cry. I understood now why she wanted to go to Japan. "I thought you made good money."

The corner of her mouth tugged into a half-smile. "I can. I used to, but it's just not really happening anymore. My days are numbered. If I don't make enough to open my shop, I'm fucked. I don't want to turn fifty with nothing to show for all the years I've sold my body."

I didn't know what to say. So I said nothing.

She looked around my pint-sized apartment. "You have a great set-up here. Don't start spending more just because you're making more. Stay grounded, and you'll never *have* to dance to pay your bills." Her brow furrowed, and for a second I got a glimpse of her real age.

"I have no plans to quit Mod. I'm saving everything I can, but even if I were making a thousand a day at the Cinema, I'd still need my job at Mod to give the appearance of a normal job to my parents."

Liberty's face relaxed into a smile. "Working at Mod is like your beard."

"My beard?" I touched my fingers to my chin.

She giggled. "Someone who's the straight partner for a gay person, whether they know it or not. Mod is your personal beard, so the world doesn't know you work at the Cinema." Liberty was always great at lightening the mood.

"That might be an unfair comparison for the gay community, but it's a fun way to think about it."

"So, you plan to keep your beard?"

It was impossible to keep from laughing. "Yes, the beard stays!"

"Good." She walked back to the sofa and collapsed onto it. "I think you should consider going to

Sebastopol to do the private show, but don't take less than six-hundred."

I wasn't sure. "I'm afraid it won't be safe."

"Your Punjabi is harmless, believe me. For a while, Allegra was seeing him outside the club."

I tried to picture the sprightly Allegra with her pixie cut sprawled on the table in front of Lucky. It didn't come easily. "Why did she stop?"

"Allegra was working her way through beauty school. She graduated just after you started."

Another girl with a plan. Was I the only one who didn't know where she was headed? "She said he was safe?"

"She was a straight-shooter. If he'd been anything more than a run-of-the-mill deviant, she'd have made sure we all knew to keep our distance."

That was helpful, but it still meant trusting the dubious affirmation of a Cinema stripper. If Liberty had been his client, I'd know it was safe, but I didn't really know Allegra. "You think I should go?"

Her blond hair swayed as she shook her head. "I didn't say you should go, I said I thought you should consider it. If it makes you uncomfortable, you don't do it. Never do anything that doesn't sit well with you."

I was only uncomfortable on the point of safety. There was no discernible difference between undressing in the Cinema and undressing in a stockroom, except for the issue of control. "Have you ever done private shows outside a club?"

"I've done the odd bachelor party, but that's it. I'll never do those again. Great money, but…wow, those can get out of hand really fast."

I wish she would go with me. "Can I split whatever he gives me and you come along?"

She reached forward and squeezed my knee. "I wouldn't take a penny from you, Lita…but I can't go. I wish I could, but I have too much to do before I leave."

My chest tightened. "I don't know what I'll do when you're gone."

Liberty lifted her hand and wagged a finger at me. "Make all the damn money you can, that's what you'll do."

CHAPTER
FOURTEEN

This was the first time I'd driven any great distance on my own. Not that seventy-five miles was a massive undertaking, but it was yet another first in a long list of them since I'd made the decision to drop out of college. When I got off the busy 101 in Cotati, I stopped to fill my gas tank and put the top down on my faithful Volkswagen Cabriolet. Cotati was the hub of Sonoma County, an entire region well known for its wines and frequently compared to its more famous neighbor to the east, Napa County. The Napa Valley might be recognized internationally for its wines and grapes, but most Bay Area residents patronized the Sonoma County wine country instead.

Even for someone with no interest in wine, the landscape was enough to make a drive along the Scenic Highway worthwhile. The wind whipped through my hair as I cruised the last eight miles, slowing slightly below the speed limit to take in the rural panorama. Orchards and farms mingled side by side with rolling vineyards and tiny antique shops, all enveloped in the heady scent of soil— and the occasional pocket of manure.

The series of postcard-worthy scenes was hampered only by my apprehension. *How could something so pleasant be wholly intertwined with something so distasteful?*

Ever the businessman, Lucky reveled in our negotiations when I'd called.

"Seven-fifty is too much for only two hours," he argued. "Stay for four."

"It's a three-hour, round-trip journey for me, plus gas, and wear and tear on my old car. If you'd rather come to the club instead, that would honestly be my preference."

After a little more hemming and hawing, the deal was struck: two hours for six-hundred-fifty dollars. He'd also promised that one of those hours would be spent fully clothed in a restaurant, enjoying a nice lunch. For a guy who had stressed this wasn't a date, he'd sure gone out of his way to make it sound like one.

And so here I was, coasting toward Sebastopol.

He had given me clear directions to his store, which was conveniently just off the highway I was already on. Like most of the surrounding entrances, his driveway began with a short gravel path before transitioning to concrete. I remembered my great-aunt's house, with its long stretch of gravel, leading to a cozy ranch-style home. Of course, I never felt this much trepidation on that driveway.

The store was small with a tired, wooden facade painted in what might have once been white but was now an ashen, sunburned sand. An older-model ice machine stood nobly by the entry door under a sign that read Mike's Market. I didn't know who Mike was, but his market looked like it might collapse under a strong gust of wind.

I parked next to a cobalt blue Corolla and turned off the ignition. Dressed for comfort in a pair of distressed boyfriend jeans and cream ballerina flats, I stepped onto the gravel with a crunch. I didn't bother putting the top up. If my car were going to be stolen from the front of a country store, I'd just as soon not have the top sliced open if it were recovered.

A bell on the door handle jingled as I pushed through.

Lucky looked up from wiping the counter with a cloth. "You came!" He sounded surprised. Perhaps after my reluctance he thought I might change my mind.

"I did. It's a beautiful drive."

"Beautiful drive for a beautiful lady."

Spare me the cheese, please. I smiled. "Thanks."

Lucky folded the rag neatly and came to the door, changing the arrows on his open sign to show he'd be back in two hours. "This is my business," he said proudly.

I let my eyes wander over the six small, cluttered aisles. If this were what he depended on for a living, it was outside the realm of my own understanding how he could possibly afford me. "It's cute." I gave him a convincing smile.

"I know it doesn't look like much, but it's more of a project than anything else. Some guy named Mike owned it before, but when he died, it went to auction. I bought it as something to do."

Well, that explained who Mike was but not much else. "This store is...your hobby?"

"Basically. I've never worked before so this sounded like a good start." Lucky was in his forties. It hardly seemed possible that he'd never worked before.

"Your first job is opening and running your own store?"

"There's some money in my family." He waved his hand, dismissing the words as they came from his mouth. "It doesn't matter." The door lock clicked. "We can go to the back."

With the clank of his keys, I suddenly felt like a caged animal. "I'm not comfortable being locked in."

Lucky walked forward and took me by the hand. Gently unfolding my tense fingers. He placed the keys in my palm. "You can go whenever you'd like." Then he brushed past me and didn't look back, instead waving for me to follow.

I did. Through a storeroom and down a corridor, we reached an old breakroom. It was sparsely furnished with a worn taupe couch, two faded oak dining chairs with duct tape holding their torn seats in place, a microwave, and a paint-splattered sink. The fluorescent light flickered sporadically and hummed above.

"You look nice in regular clothes." He muttered the words, already starting to turn back into his usual, raspy self. No matter, Lucky the customer felt more comfortable than Lucky the storekeep.

I held my right hand out, still clutching the keys. "You've filled this hand, and I thank you for that." I put my left hand forward. "But this hand is still empty."

Lucky chuckled. "All right, all right." He took a lump of folded bills from his shirt pocket and handed it to me.

"Thank you." I counted them quickly and crammed the bills into the front pocket of my jeans. I wouldn't be letting those out of my sight. "How do you want to do this?"

Lucky disappeared into the corridor, reentering with two cardboard boxes in his hands. He set them down on the floor about two feet apart and pulled forward one of the t-back dining chairs. "Can you sit in the chair and spread your legs with a foot propped on each box?" Lucky had designed a poor man's stirrups.

"I can do that. Fully nude?" I realized then that I should have brought my Cinema outfit, remembering his half-on, half-off preference.

He nodded. It didn't seem to matter to him.

I began to undress, folding my clothes and placing them carefully on the second chair. He stood in front of the sofa and watched as I peeled away each article of clothing. The room was colder than the spaces in the Cinema, and my skin started to prickle with goosebumps. My nipples were so hard they could cut ice.

"Oh God," he moaned. "I just…I have to…" He reached his hand forward, grazing his thumb against my nipple. I froze, and he quickly pulled his arm back. "Is it OK?"

Every man I danced for at the club touched my breasts. Every single one. I'd become wholly desensitized to it. I no more felt their hands on my body than I felt my own. But this? This was different. This wasn't the club, though it was still just Lucky. I needed to remember that: *It's just Lucky.* The job was the same as it would have been in the Cinema. "It's alright," I replied, perhaps a bit unconvincingly. "I'm just not used to being like this outside the club."

His Adam's apple bounced as he swallowed. This time both hands came forward, and he cupped a breast in each. He massaged gently, rubbing his thumbs over my nipples. His breathing grew heavy.

I don't think we're going to need the whole hour.

I stood while he groped me, moving his hands over my stomach and squeezing my thighs. He made no

137

attempt to press between my legs, and I soon relaxed, at ease with my surroundings.

"Do you want me to sit down now?" I asked.

He murmured incoherently, then backed away and seated himself on the couch. I sat, lifted a heel onto each box, and then reclined back in the chair, using my fingers to lightly pull my lips apart, offering full exposure.

Lucky undid his belt and slid his pants to his knees. At the club, he only pulled his dick out through the zipper of his trousers, but in his own space, he took more liberties. I didn't care, as long as he stayed seated. His little pecker bobbed in its hairy cushion, and he started stroking it. I rested my head back against the chair.

Without the cover of darkness that the Cinema provided, I could see everything Lucky did, and Lucky could see everything I did. I had to be careful not to let the boredom reflect on my face. No man was dumb enough to believe I might actually be getting off on this, but that didn't give me license to act bored—no matter how much it felt like a chore.

Lucky's panting became heavier, his mouth contorting quickly from a strained smile to a pucker; back and forth, like cheek exercises. He released a low, guttural groan, covering his paltry mushroom head with his free hand, capping the stream of fluid he expelled.

I sat quietly as his breathing stabilized, waiting to find out if there was something more he wanted to do with the rest of his time.

I didn't have to wait long.

He shrugged his shoulders. "Ready for lunch?"

CHAPTER
FIFTEEN

The following Monday I was back at the Cinema but more cautious about who was coming in and out. Liberty was right—it would be more embarrassing for almost anyone coming in to be recognized by me than the reverse. Mr. Hunter risked far more with his reputation and his position if he were outed by a former student. I had something of a reputation that could be tainted, but stripping would most likely be chalked up to youthful, teenage rebellion. I could probably depend on that, if the worst should happen.

Whatever might come to pass, for now I was going to go full-steam ahead. After an easy day in

Sebastopol and some days off from Mod, I was refreshed and ready to kick into action when I arrived for dayshift.

My little tribe of regulars had apparently missed me the week before, their faces conveying a mixture of joy and relief as each filtered in and found me working the floor. Familiar with the game, I assured each one that I'd spent the day sunbathing on a beach in Santa Cruz—far more sexy than saying I was sick and far less threatening than admitting I'd been bought out for the day.

My shift would be over after lineup in fifteen minutes, so I made a final round, lowering myself onto the lap of each man in the audience. I'd rub the outside of my knee along the inside of their thigh, leaning my breasts into their nose. "Would you like a dance?"

One by one, I was rejected. It didn't bother me anymore. I knew it was par for the course.

A new face in the back row made eye contact. I went to him.

He had on a pair of shiny nylon running shorts, and his erection poked into my knee as I made my glide.

"What's your name?" he asked. He was a smoker, not a runner.

I settled in for the tough sell and gave my sweetest smile. "Lolita."

"Ahhhh," he purred with his cigarette breath. "Are you the nymphet promised by Nabokov?"

I wouldn't know, since I've never read the book. "I am."

He exhaled heavily, and I was certain it was enough for me to absorb secondhand-smoke toxins. "You look like it. I won't ask how old you are, because I don't want you to lie to me."

It wasn't my job to psychoanalyze the fetishes of my customers, but if they were going to tell me, I had the exact opposite desire of Mr. Shiny Shorts. *I want you to lie to me.* The smile remained plastered on my face as I shifted the weight of my hip into his boner. "I think we should go in the back. It feels like you're ready."

"I think I am too, but let's go to the wall."

The wall. I hated the damn wall. "Perfect," I replied, standing up.

His hand lingered on my waist, and he walked so close behind me as we made our way to the wall that I could feel the silken rub of his shorts—and his hard-on—against the back of my thigh. He selected his spot on the wall and relaxed against it, handing me a twenty.

"Do you want me topless for forty?"

"Not today."

It was hard to see him, but he was definitely in his late-fifties. He was bald on the top of his head, just a tuft of gray that circled around the back and met with his wired glasses above the ear.

I turned my back to him and pressed gently against him, moving my body slowly. The dance wasn't really a dance. I swayed my hips, which he grabbed tightly, and arched my back, assisted by his bulging belly. The shorts seemed a bizarre fashion choice, but it became clear why he'd selected them. It was as close to skin-on-skin contact as he was going to get, and he was as much a pro as I was with this game.

As the song drew to an end, his grip on my hips became tighter. I was used to men going for a hard grind when their time was just about up, but I was painfully aware that the sheer cloth of his shorts wouldn't offer the same protection as a pair of jeans.

His movements became jerky and aggressive. Sensing what was about to come, I forcefully broke away, pushing my leg against the wall and freeing myself from his grip. I stumbled forward and caught myself on the opposing wall, turning just in time to watch a wet patch spread across the front of his shorts.

That shit would've been all over me.

I scurried away, leaving him alone with his sodden shorts and neurotic impulses. My day was over, and I was ready to go home to pizza and television. Fed up and about to enter the chute to sign out with Zakir before being forced onto the lineup, I felt a tap on my shoulder. I swirled around, expecting to see my pervert in college track shorts.

"Mark!" I gasped. It was like standing in front of a ghost. I hadn't seen Mark since the day he made me sign on as a contractor to sell lingerie. The man pulling all the strings here barely made appearances upstairs.

"Lolita." He winked and gave a sly smile. "I've heard good things about you."

I glanced to my side, trying to get a glimpse of Zakir from the corner of my eye. He pretended not to be listening, but Zakir was good at making himself invisible when it suited him. "I don't know what you've heard, but I'm happy it's good."

Mark acknowledged this with a nod. "I'm putting together the schedule for next month. Would you be interested in featuring?"

Featuring? What could I possibly offer as a feature?
"Mark, I've never done porn or worked anywhere else. I don't even like to dance on stage."

This statement appeared to catch Zakir's attention, and he offered a quick glare of warning.

I grabbed for straws. "I mean, I don't have the same stage presence as some of the other girls."

"It wouldn't matter, you wouldn't feature alone. I'm putting you up with two other girls, young like you, a 'barely legal' feature."

I let that sink in, trying to figure out what it would entail. "I can't do girl-on-girl shows, Mark. I'm really grateful for the offer, but I can't."

"Bah!" He waved his hand. "That's all for show. Forget about that. It isn't real."

It sure looked real when I saw other features who worked in pairs. "I'll have to think about it."

"The other two girls, Poppy and Brooklyn, have said yes. I'd like to have three, and Zakir tells me you have guys calling and asking for you when you're not here."

"Did he?" This time I shot the stink-eye in his direction.

Again, he pretended not to be paying attention.

Mark continued unfazed, "I don't pay in-house features, but I do waive the house fee and offer the private feature room. The three of you together will make a ton of money, all yours to keep."

That wasn't going to work without girl-on-girl action. I made a poor actress, but I'd seen the line of men for features. Mark was telling the truth about the money.

"Think about it," he continued, "but let me know soon. I have to get pictures taken for the ad."

I stepped back. "The ad?"

Mark snapped his fingers and shouted something to Zakir in their mother tongue. He walked over to the podium, and Zakir passed a newspaper to him. "This," he said, walking back and opening a copy of the San Francisco Chronicle, "this is the ad."

I took the paper gingerly. Spread out over half of the classified personals was a huge ad for the club: *Market Street Cinema presents…* with a picture of porn star Anita Dick, her purple hair piled high on top of her head and an over-sized lollipop plunged between her huge tits. "Think of all the new regulars you will get."

You mean, think of how my grandparents might see this! I handed the paper back to him. "I'm flattered, Mark…really, I am. But I can't have my picture in the Chronicle. It would destroy my family if they found out I worked here."

He folded the newspaper neatly and tucked it under his arm. "We don't need your face in the picture." He tilted his head to the side and inspected my ass with clinical detachment. "We can have the other two girls' faces and you from behind."

"That would be good!" Zakir shouted from the podium. "Have her backside in the picture with a girl on each side biting her ass." He chomped his teeth dramatically.

"Thanks for joining us, Zakir!" I couldn't help it.

He blew me a kiss.

Asshole.

"There you go," Mark said. "Problem solved."

It might be a good opportunity to make a fat bankroll that week, but I needed to talk to Liberty, get her advice. "Let me think about it, Mark. I'd have to take time off from my other job, and…I just need to think it over."

"Go on, then." He shooed me away with the back of his hand. "Go home and think. But let me know by Wednesday."

CHAPTER
SIXTEEN

"**T**his place is perfect."

Located on Cole Street in the Haight, Liberty's living room flooded with light through east-facing bay windows. All her furniture gleamed, stark white except for punches of lemon yellow on billowy curtains and throw pillows, making the Brazilian tigerwood floor pop against the crisp palette.

Liberty poured boiling water from a kettle into an antique porcelain teapot. "Sencha should pair well with the white-chocolate macadamia-nut cookies you brought."

I gazed out the window, over the treetops to the streets below. "Sencha?"

"It's a Japanese green tea. It's subtle—balances well with creamy textures and vanilla." She placed two delicate, elaborately glazed porcelain teacups on a tray and brought the service over. "You'll like it."

I moved around a white winged-back chair, stopping before taking a seat in it. "I'm kind of afraid to touch anything."

"Don't be silly! This is my home. Please, sit."

I sat, resting my hands on my lap. "I can't believe you live here."

Aside from the route to the club, I was only familiar with the tourist areas of the city. I'd spent plenty of time in Union Square, wandering around Golden Gate Park, and hitting typical spots like Ghirardelli Square and Fisherman's Warf, but the Haight was not really on my radar. Perhaps it should have been, with its boutique shops and cafes, especially Upper Haight/Cole Valley, where Liberty lived. It was so easy to get to, taking BART to Powell Street and then hopping on MUNI only ten-minutes down the line.

"I sometimes can't believe it either. This apartment is my sanctuary. No matter what troubles I've got going on outside, I forget them almost as soon as I walk through the door."

It was a beautiful notion. If it were true for her, I was glad, but my troubles followed me, even through her magnificent door. "I don't know what to do about Mark's offer to feature."

Liberty picked up a cookie and set it on an elegant, gold-rimmed plate. My wonky baked treat looked out of place in its new home. "At your age, I would have said yes."

"And now?" I didn't know how to inquire about her thoughts at her current age without pointing out the difference, which felt so much more severe in her grown-up apartment.

"Now, if I had the experience of my age but was in your position, I'd say no."

I rolled that over in my head.

Liberty took a bite from the cookie. "Oh, my gosh, Lita." She held the cookie away from her face and studied it. "These are better than the ones I buy at the pastry shop downstairs. How?"

"Thanks. It's pretty easy. I mostly follow recipes, but I play with them a lot too." I didn't dare take one myself; I'd get crumbs everywhere. "So why would you say no to featuring now?"

She set her plate down carefully and looked me straight in the eye. "You have your whole life ahead of you. Anything you do in this industry, keep it on the down low. Don't tell anyone you do it, and don't leave any trace that might link you to this down the road."

I had no intention of telling anyone, but I didn't see how a feature with a fake name and obscured picture could be linked back to me later. "How could this hurt me later if nobody knows about it now?"

"Maybe it won't. Maybe you will do this for a few years and be able to sweep it under the rug. But what if—and hear me out, however silly it sounds—what if, one day, you become famous? It could be anything. What if you happen to trip, fall, and discover a new planet? Or what if your kids grow up and one decides to become a politician?"

She was really reaching, but she had my attention.

"So, Lita becomes an overnight sensation or her daughter grows up and runs for President of the United States. Do you think the press, with all of their resources, won't dig this up and run it on the front page?"

Now she really had my full attention.

"You have to be careful. You have to be smart. You're in this situation now and making the best of it—

and, frankly, you're doing an amazing job—but don't get sloppy. Don't forget this situation is temporary. If you want to say it doesn't matter, I get it—it never mattered to me either—but if you want kids, think about how your choices might impact their lives down the line."

I couldn't do anything but stare at her. My mouth was dry, and the hair was standing up on the back of my neck. Liberty, in her fancy apartment, with more wisdom in her pinky finger than I had in my entire body, had just given me the best advice anyone could have provided. "You are the greatest friend I've ever had."

"I'll always be that friend to you, and I hope you'll be that for me."

"I will," I promised. Sad she was leaving, I no longer questioned her judgment on it. "Are you finished packing?"

"Almost done!" She stood up from the couch. "Come help me with a couple things?"

We passed through a pair of French doors leading into her bedroom. The decor carried over from one room to the next, except the fresh yellow accents gave way to a soft sage green. Two heavy suitcases were stacked on top of a shaggy flokati area rug. A cosmetic bag overflowed on the dresser, its contents jutting out in every direction. "I don't think you're going to be able to close that."

"I'm not leaving any of them behind! I'll need my entire arsenal and then some." Liberty opened one of the drawers. "I hope you don't mind, but I gave the landlord your name and phone number as my emergency contact."

I was flattered. "Of course I don't mind!" I had given Patty my parent's phone number. As alone as I always thought I was, it turned out Liberty was more so.

She felt around the back of the drawer. "I know there's another one back there." Her eyes lit up. "Got it!" Liberty withdrew a brass key strung on a bit of lace and handed it to me. "I keep all my documents and important things in a lockbox in the back of the closet. Take this in case I get to Japan and need something else, like if the landlord asks for something. You just never know."

Gaping at her huge suitcases, I asked, "What more could you possibly need?"

She shrugged. "I don't know but just in case. I keep a copy of my passport in there, my birth certificate, all that. Maybe I'll lose my purse on the *Tokaido Shinkansen* and need you to fax copies to the embassy. Maybe I get robbed. Maybe I drink too much and leave my bag in the bathroom of a bar. Just please, keep it."

"And how do I get into the apartment?"

She took a second key from the top of the dresser. "You use this."

I snatched the key from her hand. "I'm going to move in here and never leave!"

"Come whenever you'd like!" She raised her arms and bowed. *"Mi casa estu casa."*

I laughed. "I don't think Spanish is going to get you very far in Japan!"

Liberty walked toward me and wrapped her arms around me. It felt so good to have a friend who trusted me unreservedly, whom I could trust the same way. As an only child, this was how I always imagined it would be to have a big sister. "I'm going to miss you so much."

Her forehead pressed against my temple. "I'm going to miss you too." She pulled away. "Don't do the feature. You'll regret it."

I knew she was right. "I'm not going to do it."

"And promise me—" Her eyes glazed over with the gleam of tears. "Promise me you'll find your calling and get out of this business soon."

I wished I knew how long that would take. "I don't have a crystal ball, Liberty."

"Just don't fall into the same trap I did. Don't wait ten or twenty years before you start making decisions in your life."

I understood what she meant, even if I had no idea how I would keep my word. "I promise."

We stood silently, sniffling. Neither shed a tear, but we both choked up. Six weeks wasn't very long, but it felt like an eternity when she was the only person I could talk to.

We said our goodbyes, and I left with a heavy heart, taking MUNI back to Powell Street. Before leaving the city, I watched the cable cars load and make a couple of turnarounds while I noshed on a slice of Blondie's pizza. The flavors melted in my mouth, gooey cheese with the sweet kick of tomato sauce. The crust had a little crunch to it, balancing out the slight oiliness. I didn't have much of an appetite, but I couldn't visit the city and skip my favorite part.

Yet the city seemed different than I remembered. San Francisco, this incredible metropolis by the bay, now had a shadow over it in my heart. I had always ridden in with excitement, but nowadays the trips were a bit ominous. I wasn't exactly innocent before I began working at Market Street Cinema, but I could never have imagined the direction my life had taken.

On Powell, I turned toward the intersection with Market Street. The Cinema was still a ways down, but I felt it reaching for me, grabbing me. The city had been one of my favorite, happiest spots, but now all I could feel was the Cinema sucking the life from me.

CHAPTER
SEVENTEEN

I finally called Mom back and set up a lunch date. Liberty's isolation, her admission that I was the closest thing she had to family in case of an emergency, forced me to see how fortunate I was to have a persistent mother. If real trouble came, I had people who would help me. My situation in life was my choice; I could choose to leave stripping at any moment. Maybe Liberty had also chosen her path, but unlike me, she was now on a one-way street, still far from where she wanted to be. And she was running out of time.

As lunchtime grew close, I slid the straps of yet another netted, baby-doll nighty onto yet another of Mod's miniature hangers. "Don't forget I'm taking an hour lunch today instead of thirty minutes."

"When have I ever forgotten anything?" Amelia inspected my work and nodded approvingly. "I'm glad you've patched things up with your mother."

I picked up the next nighty. "I wouldn't say patched up, but I'm ready to make nice. And you forget many things."

She took the tidy collection of hung lingerie and moved it to a rolling rack. "I haven't forgotten that, after months of asking, you still haven't told me if you're interested in being my assistant manager."

I hadn't forgotten, but I didn't understand why she was pestering me to become an assistant manager. This store had three employees but just enough work for one. "I don't know, Amelia. I haven't decided yet."

She pushed the rack to the side, releasing a sigh. That could've been caused by my answer, but it also could've been the result of exertion. Pushing the racks was just about the only exercise she'd been getting for some time. "This thing is heavy."

I gave it a light shove, and it rolled with hardly any effort.

"See why you're needed here?" she joked.

"She's needed for lunch!" Mom strolled in, placing her sunglasses on top of her head. "Hi, honey."

"Mom, you remember Amelia?"

"Of course I do! Amelia has been wonderfully patient with my messages for you." She extended her hand.

Amelia took it firmly into her own. "From one mother to another, I understand."

"Thank you," Mom replied.

"I've offered Lita an assistant manager's position, if she'll take it."

I could feel a fluttering in my stomach. "Is that public information, Amelia?" I didn't know what my mother's reaction would be, either encouraging me to take a job I didn't have the drive to do well or discouraging me since she never wanted me to work at Mod in the first place.

"Ah, telling a mother isn't the public!" Amelia winked.

Mom's face lit up. "This might be the first opportunity for me to declare my intent to step aside. Lita is running her own show. . . she can decide."

I almost fell to the floor. *Lita is running her own show?* Who was this woman?

"She's a good girl. Clever," Amelia conceded. "You did a good job."

"OK, OK!" This tete-a-tete between the mothers was about to end. It was confusing and embarrassing. I took my purse from behind the counter and threw the strap over my shoulder. "Let's get some food, Mom."

"Thanks again, Amelia," she called back as I tugged her out the door.

Once we were safely in the swarm of the mall, I stopped and let go of her arm. "What exactly did you mean when you said that I'm running my own show?"

Her attention shifted to the crinkled elbow of her blouse. "I just had this dry cleaned."

I brushed the rumpled sleeve with my hand, trying half-heartedly to smooth the wrinkles. "Sorry, Mom."

She dismissed the apology. "Forget it, it's fine. I'm just happy you called."

I was happy I did too, but that didn't answer my question. "Seriously Mom, what did you mean by that?"

"I don't want to push you away, Lita." She shifted from one leg to the other uncomfortably. "I feel like I pushed you away." Her guilt was palpable, and it ate away at me. They might have pushed me out of the nest, but that wasn't why I had been avoiding her.

"You didn't push me away, Mom. I really have been very busy."

She swallowed hard, and her eyes went a little misty. She didn't believe me. When I started to walk, she hesitated as if she were afraid that, if she moved from the spot where she stood, the conversation would remain forever unfinished.

That had been my intent, but I could see it wouldn't work this time. The wince in the fine lines around her eyes spoke of such pain, and her crestfallen expression left my heart broken too. "You haven't pushed me away, Mom." It came out barely above a whisper. "I promise."

My assurance satisfied her enough to get us moving again. We weaved our way through women pushing strollers and handholding couples with bulging shopping bags. The hum of voices carried over the generic music pouring from the shops, and kids screamed and giggled from the play areas in the distance. It offered just enough of a distraction to keep the silence between us tolerable. We hadn't even agreed on where we were going, but at this point, it was safe to assume that Mom's appetite had been obliterated by melancholy, just as mine had. In almost a trance, we ended up in front of the same Tex-

Mex restaurant I'd been in when she'd interrupted my lunch the last time we'd met.

It felt like ages ago.

I looked to her. "I've missed you, Mom."

She fought back tears, offering me a tight smile that was wholly sincere but restrained just enough to prevent her eyelids from spilling over.

I reached forward and again brushed my hand over the crumpled mess I'd made of her sleeve. "I should have called you."

Her lips went into a pucker, and she pulled me into her arms, holding me there until she believed I wasn't going to push away this time. We stood in that embrace, quietly forgiving each other—although I couldn't yet forgive myself.

When she released me, we walked into the restaurant. She gazed up at the menu on the back wall, but a quick flurry of motion from a nearby table caught my eye.

I turned.

And I almost threw up.

My Chinese daddy rubbed his eyes in a way that assured me he had seen me also and then tried to hide his face behind his hands.

My heart leapt up into my throat. I glanced nervously to my mom, who was still studying the menu, oblivious to the dire collision of my professional and private lives.

I decided to peek back to his table. He was seated with an Asian woman, close to his age, with a short, rollered hairstyle and a yellow puffy jacket. She barked in Mandarin to a young boy of about twelve hopping on and off the chair next to her. To his right were two girls, one about my age and one that couldn't have been more than a year or two younger. The older wore her hair pulled back in a loose, long ponytail, while the younger kept hers in a sleek, chin-length bob.

He turned so we made eye contact. His face drained of all color, then his eyes darted to his wife in a frenzied plea.

He was terrified of me.

I had been terrified of him, but just as Liberty had promised, he had more at stake than I did. I continued to stare. This man had daughters my age. Week after week, I sat naked on his lap while he poked and prodded my body, insisting that I call him daddy.

My horrified gaze landed on the girls. What if it weren't just a daddy fetish? What if he was trying to control some twisted—?

The older girl tilted her head in my direction. Her eyes held no clue as to what her life at home might be like, but they stared at me in curiosity. From behind, her father gave me a pleading look, biting his lower lip and wiping away a bead of sweat from his temple with the back of his hand.

Stifling my shock, I turned to my mom. "Someone told me that the restaurant inside Nordstrom now does an afternoon tea service. Want to go there instead?"

Her eyes widened. "Oh! That sounds like fun!"

"Let's try it."

We exited the restaurant, but as we passed by the last window, I glanced through to the table. While her father had relaxed, relieved of his fears, the girl continued to watch me with inquisitive raised brows until I stepped out of view.

Our exchange didn't go unnoticed. "Do you know that girl?" Mom asked casually.

I tucked a stray hair behind my ear. "I don't know the girl, but her father has bought some things from me before." It was the truth, even if I were misleading my mother.

"Oh, that's pretty gross, Lita." She shook her hands like she'd touched something dirty. "You know how I feel about you and that store. Everyone needs to buy underwear somewhere, but those men buying that type of lingerie from my baby—I just don't want to even think about it."

She had absolutely no idea what types of things *those men* were buying from *her baby*. And I intended to keep it that way.

CHAPTER
EIGHTEEN

"Thank you so much!" He shoved a wad of cash into my hands. "Thank you!"

I straightened the bills. I didn't take the time to count them because it didn't matter. This wasn't for a dance; this was a payoff. "You don't need to worry about me making a scene. I don't do that." I folded the stack neatly and put it in my wristlet.

My Chinese daddy dropped into the chair. "I almost had a heart attack!"

I fixed my eyes on him blankly. Maybe a heart attack wouldn't be such a bad thing in this case. "Were those your kids?"

His face transformed from intense relief to embarrassment. "It's not what you think."

I continued to stare, expressionless.

He shuffled in the chair. "It's not like that at all. It's just a fantasy. I don't really want that!"

In the porn room, plenty of daddy-play and age-play flashed across the big screen. I knew men came here to let their imaginations roam to the dark places they would never stray to in real life, but I couldn't shoulder the huge burden of trusting him or anyone who came in and chose a dance from me obviously based on my age. I had enough guilt on my conscience from keeping my family at arm's length. This club had turned out to be a real funhouse.

He grew more flustered by the second. "I swear it! God—this is all just a kind of *Dom* fantasy!"

I knew the difference. I had been here long enough to see that the gray areas weren't actually that gray since we were, ultimately, all consenting adults—at least in here. In the end I could only hope he was telling the truth. I wasn't judging him for having an age-play fantasy, but I did have the right to turn down anyone for any reason. I couldn't play my role with him anymore. His kids made it too personal.

My Chinese daddy would be *persona non grata* in my cubicles from now on.

"There's two other girls here, Poppy and Brooklyn. You'll like them. Maybe go to the front and ask Zakir when they're working. They'll be featuring a barely legal show on stage next month." I had turned the feature down, but they were still grabbing the opportunity.

He didn't argue and stood up quickly. "Poppy and Brooklyn?"

I held the curtain back to aid in his escape. "Either...or both. They do dances together."

His eyebrows shot up. Christmas had come early.

I hung back for a minute after he'd left to count the cash he'd handed me: *Twenty, forty, sixty, eighty...* When I finished counting, I couldn't believe it, six hundred dollars—almost what he paid for a month of indulgence—for walking away quietly.

"Knock, knock."

"Liberty!" I leapt toward her voice and threw my arms around her neck.

"Hey, cutie." She sounded tired. Sad.

I let go so I could study her. Her eyes sparkled like her smile, but they didn't curve up at the corners. "What are you doing here? Why aren't you in Japan?"

She eyed the chair, trying to decide under the red light if it were safe. I grabbed a handful of clean tissues, moistened them with hand sanitizer from the dispenser on the outer wall, and then swabbed the seat down. "Hang on, let me dry it off."

"Forget it," Liberty replied, plopping down. "The backs of my legs could use the sanitizing anyways."

Happy, confused, even a little worried, I could hardly believe she was right in front of me. "What happened?"

She started to relax her head against the back of seat but quickly remembered where she was and sat up straight. "Ew," she mumbled.

"Liberty, what happened?"

She discharged an exaggerated sigh as her stripper facade fell away. "It was a fucking mess." She leaned back, abandoning any sanitation concern she'd had seconds before.

From the black cubicle behind me, I pulled forward a chair, wiped it down briskly, and planted myself on it. "Talk to me. Please."

Her body drooped forward, and she dropped her elbows to her knees, cradling her face in her hands. "What am I going to do now?"

"Oh, Liberty." I caressed the side of her slender arm. Her shoulders started to shake. "Please, don't cry."

Her breath caught in her throat, releasing a faint sob. "There's nothing left for me." While she sobbed softly, her tears rolled gently from her palms to drop from her wrists.

I stood and moved behind her, rubbing her back gently with my hand. I didn't know what to say to her, and I didn't want to push her further with questions. Whatever it was, it couldn't have been good. She was always so full of light, so positive, and she shared her light with me. Now, her agony was my own, and I felt her deep despair.

I grabbed another tissue, this time pressing it lightly against her fingertips. She pulled her hands from her face and took the tissue. After dabbing her eyes and blowing her nose, she smiled feebly. "I think I'm going to have to do my make-up again."

I sat back in my chair. "We can stay here until you're ready."

"You know, I went all the way there to take the class in Kyoto and earn some cash at the club."

I sat silently as she blew her nose.

"I went to Tokyo first and met with someone who worked at the club, but the manager wasn't there. He told

173

me to come back the next day, but I already had a ticket to Kyoto and arrangements to meet with the person I would be renting a room from there during the week."

She took a deep breath, steadying herself. "The manager knew I was coming to work the following weekend, so I thought nothing of it. I got on the train and went to Kyoto—which is magical, by the way."

I gave her an easy smile. Of course, in all this she still saw the good.

"I dropped off my luggage in my room, made my way to the school, signed, paid the fees, yada, yada. I spent the rest of the week just exploring this new, fascinating city."

"Did you not start at the school right away?"

She shook her head. "It didn't start until the week after. I went back to Tokyo on Friday morning to get settled into the dancer's dormitory, a place set up by the club, but I didn't care because it was only a couple nights a week. And Tokyo is crazy expensive—even more than here."

I had watched a documentary on the capsule hotels there. Any place that could charge fifty dollars a night to sleep in a pod must be astronomical.

"I go to the dorm, I get ready, and I go with the girls to the club. The manager is there, obviously, because I wasn't the only new girl, and we had to sign some things." She dropped her head back into her hands and rocked it back and forth. "He told me I couldn't work. He said I was too old."

"That asshole…" My blood boiled at the thought. "Fucking asshole."

Liberty lifted her head and fought back a new rush of tears.

"There weren't other clubs?" There had to be dozens in Tokyo alone.

"I went to one other that I knew was safe. Same thing. Too old. And I won't work at a club that nobody has vouched for. Too many things can go wrong. That's how girls end up being trafficked."

It was a dirty, scary world out there, but this hit way too close to home. "Thank God you didn't try out of desperation."

"I just bought a return ticket and came straight home." She bobbed her shoulders sluggishly. "But there's nothing for me here either. I'm not making enough to live. My rent alone is forcing me into my savings, and I need every penny—and more—to get to the next step."

Her teahouse. If she wasn't saving anymore, if she was actually spending her savings, she would never open her shop. "You can get there, Liberty."

"I can't. It's too late."

There had to be a way. In the few months I had been working at the Cinema, I spent everything I earned at Mod but saved everything I earned here, thousands, more than I could have saved at Mod in years. "You can, Liberty. Let me help."

She brushed her fingers across my knee. "You're very sweet, but nobody can help me."

"I can," I insisted. "We can get an apartment together outside the city and split the rent. If we just reduce your expenses and figure out—"

"It won't be enough, Lita."

"It will!" I knew it would. And I could help her; we could even cosign on a business loan if we had to. Surely we had enough combined capital to—

"I need to get out there and make my quota. Your shift is almost over, but mine is just beginning. Let me get through tonight, and I'll call you later this week."

"Alright, Liberty." Tonight I'd plan how this would work. And it would work. "Call me."

She hugged me tight, and I squeezed back, wishing to draw the pain away from her. It wasn't hopeless. She'd see that. I'd have the financials worked out, every penny we'd need and where we could get it.

"I love you," she whispered.

"I love you too."

Everything is going to be fine.

CHAPTER
NINETEEN

I spent that evening and the next couple days drawing up plans. My coffee table was littered with yellow lined tablet paper, each sheet bearing figures for different scenarios. Each had a blank because I didn't know what she'd saved herself, but we could sort that out when we talked.

The neat array of pages ran the gauntlet of every possible idea I could rack from my brain, including the prospect of me enrolling in a pastry program. It was just a trade course, but the more I considered it, the more I liked the idea. I could even appeal to my parents on the grounds that it was, technically, college. From that angle, I could enlist their help in paying my half of the rent. Then I could split Liberty's half and continue working at the Cinema on Mondays, continue saving until we could open her shop. By then maybe I'd be trained to make the fancy cookies and cakes she wanted to serve, but I certainly wouldn't press her into hiring me.

I'd lend her what I'd saved out of love, simply because I wanted her to succeed.

She'd accept at least a few of the apartments I'd found, I was certain. None were in San Francisco, but they all kept to the nicer areas of the East Bay. I had high hopes for a place I'd found in San Ramon, a lovely two bedroom in a hillside complex right off of Crow Canyon Road. Fingers crossed, I hoped she'd liked it too.

But I had to get ahold of her first.

Her home phone always clicked to the answering machine on the fourth ring. I'd left so many messages that, after the beep, the call just dropped. By Thursday, I decided to call the club.

I spent the morning at Mod, cleaning and stocking. Amelia lurked in the back office doing paperwork, which meant she was watching soap operas on a nineteen-inch TV she kept stashed in a locking armoire. She made her fair share of personal calls, yapping away in rapid Spanish, so I doubted she would care if I made a call, as long as I finished my work. Still, I didn't want her coming out while I was calling a San Francisco strip club, asking if a specific dancer was working. I couldn't see explaining that away very easily.

Finally, she came out. "Ok, Lita, I'm calling it a day." She had her purse slung over her shoulder and her coat folded over an arm.

"Have a great afternoon, Amelia." The clock assured me Sandra wouldn't be in for another fifteen minutes.

Amelia waved as she walked. "Will do."

I watched her round figure disappear into the mall, then lifted the phone from its cradle. On the days I wanted to work, I had to call in by ten a.m. to let them know, so I dialed the number from memory.

The ring purred in my ear.

Once.

Twice.

Three times.

I was about to hang up—

"Market Street Cinema." The phone was right in front of Zakir, yet he still took his sweet time.

"It's Lolita."

"Lolita! Too early to call for nightshift. Call back at six."

I heard a rustling. "Zakir! Zakir, wait!" I was terrified that, if he hung up, I might not be able to get him back on the line. More rustling. "Hello?"

"I'm here," he replied. "Busy, so hurry up."

My heart raced. "Is Liberty working today?"

"Liberty? No Liberty. Haven't seen her for days."

I squeezed the handset. "Not at all? Since when?"

"Monday."

"Can you have her call me if she comes in?" I hoped he'd remember but knew he wouldn't.

"Yeah, yeah. Tell Liberty to call Lolita. Got it."

"Thank—"

The phone clicked and went dead.

I didn't know what to do, but I knew I couldn't stay here. I went to the back and grabbed my coat, slipping it on so I could leave the moment Sandra appeared. The minutes ticked by, and with each clack of the hand across the dial, I became more anxious.

Sandra strolled in coolly, her dirty-blond hair tucked behind a red headband. It matched her belt and shoes, a favored accessory trio she wore several days a week.

"I have to go," I stated, grabbing my bag. "There's been an emergency. I'm sorry." I rushed out before she had a chance to ask any questions.

After running to the parking lot and jumping into my car, I endured a manic drive home. I took the frontage road to avoid the possibility of hitting traffic on the 580. Usually a careful driver, I firmly believed that the speed limit was, in fact, the absolute limit. Today I urged my little engine to flex its muscles and accelerate, hoping with every mile I wouldn't hit a damn speed trap. A normal twenty-five minute drive took less than fifteen, and I had decided, if there were no return call from Liberty on my answering machine, I'd take her key and go to her apartment.

The machine flashed red indicating a message.

I pressed play.

"Hi, um—" The machine crackled. I didn't recognize his voice. "Your number was left by Darcy in case of an emergency—" The name confused me for a second.

Oh God. Oh God, no. Darcy was Liberty's real name. "I need you to call me back. My number is—"

Pausing the message, I hurried to the opposite counter to grab a pen. Screw the paper, I hit play and scratched the numbers across my hand. Then, phone in hand, I punched in each number carefully since I thought I might throw up.

"Lita!" Patty shrieked my name, almost a blood-curdling scream. "Lita, come up here!"

Two numbers short, I slammed the phone down and ran into the hallway. She stood with the front door open, but whoever was behind it was obscured.

"Liberty!" Relief flooded over me. It had to be her. "Oh, thank God! Liberty!" I bounded up the stairs, taking two at a time.

Patty pulled the front door open as wide as it would stretch.

I stopped in my tracks at the landing.

Standing at the door was my father, his face haggard with the most sullen expression. Next to him stood a police officer.

"Oh, Lita…" Patty said, dropping heavily on a carpeted step.

"What's going on, Daddy?" I asked the question, but I knew. I knew what was going on.

Dad cleared his throat. "I'm so sorry, sweetheart."

I needed to hear it. I needed the words to make it real. "Tell me," I whispered. "Tell me, please."

The police officer stepped forward. "Your friend Darcy, she gave your name and number to her landlord. We've been trying to call you all morning, but when we couldn't get ahold of you, we traced your name back to your parents address."

"Just tell me what happened." *Tell me before I faint.*

"Sweetheart, your friend Darcy—" My dad reached up with his hand to take me in, but I stood too far back. His hand dropped limply back to his side. "Your friend Darcy…she hanged herself." His graying eyebrows twitched above watery, bloodshot eyes. "She's gone, baby."

CHAPTER
TWENTY

I had no choice but to admit how I knew Liberty. Though I answered the police officer's questions while Dad went home to collect Mom and bring her back, there was no way around telling them everything. And I didn't care. I was done lying, I was done being ashamed. I only felt an agonizing grief that threatened to paralyze my whole body as I collapsed into a chair. My best friend, my sister, had taken her own life. No negative reaction they might have at the revelation—and they most certainly would have a negative reaction—could distract me from the pain that threatened to drown me. If I thought it would distract me, even momentarily, I'd have told my father before he left. The respite a fight would have offered, however fleeting, I desperately wanted.

In my basement room with me, the police officer showed no reaction, taking notes as I answered his inquiries. He was polite, displaying the conciliatory sympathy required of his profession in these circumstances, but he offered nothing more.

"You are a dancer at the Market Street Cinema?"

"I am. I work on Mondays, always dayshift."

Scribble, scribble. "How did you meet Darcy?"

"I'm sorry, can I call her Liberty? I didn't know her as Darcy."

He nodded. *Scribble, scribble.*

"I met her when she came into Mod Unmentionables. That's where I work Tuesday to Saturday." *It's my beard.*

"She came in to buy something?"

"Yes," I answered. My head spun; it was hard to remember the exact details. "Then she invited me to the Cinema."

He raised an eyebrow. "She…invited you?"

"To sell lingerie. Soon after, though, I started to work there."

"As a dancer?"

"Yes."

Scribble, scribble. "And—" He flipped through his notepad but looked like he did it more out of habit than actually seeking anything. "When did you become close enough to be named her emergency contact?"

"Almost immediately. We were close from the second meeting. When I went to the Cinema the first time, I trusted her enough to go there, but I don't know when she started really trusting me." *She's gone now, though. She's gone.*

"You have a key to her apartment?"

It hid somewhere in the bottom of my handbag, next to the brass key on lace. "Yes."

Scribble, scribble. "When did she give it to you?"

"The day before she left for Japan."

"Japan?"

"She was going there to work, but when she arrived they told her she was too old. She came back." *And then she killed herself.*

He tapped his pen against the notepad. "She left a note."

She left a note? Where was this note? "Can I see it?"

"We can't give you the actual note until the coroner's report comes back and we've officially ruled this

189

as a suicide." Genuine tenderness shone is his gaze. "But I'll see what I can do to get you a copy. You've been named in the note as her executer and beneficiary."

She named me in her note? She mentioned me in her suicide note? "What does that mean?"

"A suicide note isn't a legally binding document, but it doesn't look like she had any next of kin. If anyone comes forward—a mother, sister, father, whoever—they could dispute it, but that's unlikely, especially since she clearly appointed you, however terrible the circumstances."

I had no reply. The room listed to the left, spinning.

"I'll call you if I have any questions. The investigation won't take more than a day or two, then the landlord will have you come in and take her things. At least the things you want. I think he plans to call a removal company to dispose of the rest."

The landlord is just going to throw her things away? All of Liberty's beautiful things? "I'll take everything."

"Great," he said, standing up, his smile just a bit too cheery. "I'll make sure a copy of the note is left in the apartment, although by the time you get in there, we might not need the original anymore."

I wanted to stand up, but I didn't have the strength.

"I'll see myself out." He walked to my door, pausing before going through it. "I'm sorry for your loss."

As he closed the door behind him gently, I collapsed into a fit of tears.

Heaving, Dad hurried to my little bathroom. I felt like vomiting too.

"You went there?" Mom asked. "Took costumes?"

I heard Dad heave again. He only had to hear how we'd met to understand everything completely. Mom was either in denial or even more naive than I ever considered.

"Mom, forget that part. Mom?"

Unasked questions remained inscribed across her face.

"Mom, listen." When her lips stopped forming questions and her eyes held steady on me, I steeled my nerve. "I've been working as a dancer at a club in San Francisco."

"A dancer? Like—?"

"Like a stripper." I didn't have the energy to tiptoe around the subject.

Dad, still hunched over the toilet, slammed the bathroom door shut. He'd heard enough.

Mom's lip began to quiver. "With your—?" She hovered her hands over her chest.

"Everything," I replied, hovering my own hands at my hips. The truth, they deserved nothing less.

"Oh, God." She choked on a sob. "Oh, dear God."

It was a knee-jerk response to the news, calling for a deity my parents didn't talk to regularly. If you asked my dad what religion he was, he'd answer *academic*.

"Why?" she asked.

"I needed the money." *Why else?*

The toilet flushed, and Dad emerged from the bathroom. He still looked pallid, but I doubted anything was left to bring up. "I don't want to hear more about this. Stop asking her questions."

"But we need to—"

"We don't need to know," Dad interrupted. "We need to move forward."

Pragmatic as always, Dad made decisions based on facts, not emotion. However much my actions had wounded him, he was ready to pull up our bootstraps and crack on.

He sat next to Mom and leaned forward toward me. "It's time to come home, Lita."

"I am home, Dad."

His glare didn't waver. "You understand what I mean, sweetheart. We love you, and we take responsibility for this, and it's time to come home."

Take responsibility for what? For the dancing? For me making a friend that I grew to love? Take responsibility for what? "Nothing here is your fault." I meant it. I made my choices, and that wasn't going to change now. "And I want to keep living on my own."

Mom slouched in her chair, looking entranced with a dull gaze.

Dad's face grew even more forlorn. "I will be destroyed if you go back to that place, Lita."

"I'm not going to go back." I could never go back. I didn't feel I'd done anything wrong by working there, but the Cinema had sucked the life out of my friend. My only regret was that I didn't understand the depth of Liberty's pain until it was too late. I would never go back.

Mom flickered back to life. "Then what will you do? How will you live?" She slumped back as soon as the words slipped from her mouth.

"I have money saved. I'll be fine." I was too broken to go back to work at Mod tomorrow, but the job would be there for me when I was ready. I had lived within my means then; I could carry on doing so now. It was a stretch on my finances, and I'd have to dip into my savings every month to stay comfortable—but I would never go back to dancing, and I wasn't moving back in with my parents.

"No," Dad replied.

"No?" I questioned. "What's no?"

"I'm going to sort out your rent with Patty. You keep working at Mod and saving from *those* wages while you decide what you want to do. I don't care what that is. If you want to be a drummer, we'll get you lessons. If you want to be a doctor, we'll get you back into college. If you want to work for one of these web things, I don't know, some internet company? That's OK too. Whatever you want to do, we support you."

I leapt off the sofa and into my father's arms. I didn't need their money for rent, and I wasn't going to take it. No, what I truly needed—all I ever needed—he gave freely with three short words: *we support you.*

CHAPTER
TWENTY-ONE

The yellow caution tape had been ripped from one edge of the door, leaving it fluttering at one side from the vent above. I had put Liberty's house key onto the same string of lace that held the brass key, and it slid easily into its lock, clicking the bolt open. I pushed through, into the light from the bay windows that engulfed her living room. I walked in, closing the door behind me. The quiet was eerie, broken only by the hum of the ventilation system.

Just as I remember.

It hadn't been more than a couple weeks since the first and only time I'd set foot in the apartment, but my whole world had changed from that day to this one.

Everything was perfectly clean. If it weren't for the caution tape outside, there'd be no clue that a few hours earlier this had been a crime scene. It even smelled the same, like bergamot and lavender. But it wasn't the same. This was no longer Liberty's home.

I walked slowly to a piece of paper folded neatly on the kitchen counter, sandwiched between a stainless-steel tin and a blank notepad. I knew exactly what it was. I wondered if she'd left it there and the officer had carefully replaced it, or if he had just decided that the countertop was the most practical place to leave it.

I ran my fingertips over the paper's grainy surface. The page creased gently where the pen had pressed against it, leaving raised, smooth loops on its underside. This was the original. I unfolded it and stared blankly at the note. I had only seen Liberty's handwriting on scratches of paper when she handed off her number, but I recognized her script. She had written this, there was no question.

My eyes began to well up, and I held the letter at a distance, terrified of smearing the ink with my tears. I was torn, not wanting to read her last words but needing to. Her voice mattered. She took her life but had something she needed to say first, and that mattered.

I walked with the note to the winged-back chair I'd been afraid to sit in but changed my mind when I got there. Instead, I went to the place on the sofa she'd seated herself. The place where she said, "This is my home."

I opened her letter:

Dear Lita,

I'm sorry.

I'm sorry for having you go to the Cinema, and I'm sorry for suggesting you try dancing. I'm sorry I brought you into a world I desperately wanted out of, and I'm sorry I abandoned you when I couldn't do it anymore. The last thing I said to you was that I loved you, and I meant it. I lost twenty years selling myself for a dream, having nothing to show for it when my time was up. I started my journey with the same optimism you have, even if you don't see it in yourself. A need to spread your wings and soar, unshackled by the expectations placed on us by others. I never made it to my destination, but you will.

Everything I have is yours. Pick up where I left off. Make a life for yourself, taking all I offer and turning it into anything you want with the time you have left.

My journey is over, but yours has only just begun.

Follow your heart.

I'll meet you on the other side.

Love Always,
Liberty

There was an inscription on the bottom clarifying her full legal name and naming me, as the officer had stated, her executor. The postscript was an obvious afterthought. It made me sad to think, after pouring her heart out onto the page, she felt the need to go back and add an impromptu will to her final words.

I took the brass key to her bedroom. Later, I would put stickers on everything I wanted the movers to bring—and I was taking it all—but that lockbox wouldn't be left behind for them. From behind a stack of sweaters in the closet, I pulled it out and sat with it on the edge of her bed.

The lock was wobbly in its casting, but with a couple back-and-forth twists, it finally opened. Her passport, birth certificate, lease agreement, and a handful of other legal documents sat on top. I sifted through, finding old photos of her as a child, and others of what could be her parents.

At the bottom was a notebook, which I opened. It was full of notes Liberty had taken, describing, in her own hand, hundreds of different tea varieties, their origin, their flavors, and pairing recommendations. I flipped through the pages, and an envelope fluttered to my lap.

An envelope with my name written on the front.

I lifted it out, turning it over in my hand. It was sealed, but only where the point of the flap met the casing.

I slid my index finger under it, releasing the glue with a quick snap.

Its contents were slim.

I unfolded them.

On top, a flyer for an intensive sixteen-week baking and pastry program in San Francisco. It read, "Our Consecutive Bread, Viennoiserie and Pastry Professional Series prepares students who would like to become a Baker and/or Pastry Chef to advance in their career. Take the next step toward opening a bakery or working in the baking industry."

Underneath the flyer was a printed receipt for the tea course Liberty had paid for in Kyoto.

The final page was a bank statement, with a letter attached showing she had made me her beneficiary. It was dated for the day after I'd last seen her at the Cinema.

The balance was in the tens of thousands—plenty to open a small shop. I glanced around her bedroom, decorated down to the last expensive detail, and knew why she didn't think she had enough. She probably only had half of what she required to meet her own standard. Liberty didn't half-ass anything.

I stared at the page and thought my heart might rip in two.

If only she'd talked to me. If only she'd waited. If we added my savings to hers, we could have opened her shop in less than a year.

I lay back onto her bed, curled into the fetal position, and cried until there was nothing left.

CHAPTER
TWENTY-TWO

"**A**re you sure you want to do this alone?" Dad gripped the steering wheel with such force that his knuckles had turned white.

My forehead was pressed against the window, the cool glass soothing where a headache had throbbed for weeks. It felt better now, but the glass reminded me it used to be there. "I'm sure."

Mom craned her neck back. "Don't worry, honey. We'll follow all your instructions."

I trusted my dad with the contractors more than I trusted my mom, but it was nice that she wanted to help however she could.

Cars whipped around us, occasionally honking before speeding past. Dad had taught me how to drive, and I learned my speed limit theory from him.

"You have everything?" It was the hundredth time she'd asked.

"Yes, Mom, I have everything."

"Call us when you get there so we know you're OK."

I'd be calling at least twice a week to check on the construction progress. "I will."

We lapsed into a comfortable silence, and I stared blindly at nothing in particular, tracing the blur of trees with my fingers.

I was tired. The grieving process had been completely foreign to me, and it took several days before I was ready to even get out of bed. When I finally pulled myself upright, I was absolutely useless. My mother came to see me every day, and I ended up giving her a key, which I regretted the second my senses were fully restored. She brought food and tidied up, a completely unnecessary chore since I only moved from the bed to the sofa, with occasional trips to the bathroom; there was nothing to clean, except myself.

Even so, I'd only bathed when Mom insisted. "Take a shower. You'll feel better," she'd urged.

I didn't.

I was also excited. Not then, but now. The greatest blessing of living on my own was the freedom and space to think. In between fits of tears and the sleep that usually accompanied it, there were moments of reflection. Ultimately, once the fog began to thin and things started to become clear, I was able to plan.

Out of all the things I'd been given by Liberty, I treasured her notebook the most, partly because it was written in her own hand and partly because it housed the details of what she enjoyed best. Her notebook had become my lifeline. I read it over and over, absorbing as much as I could, bits of her and what she loved, until I was ready to leave the house.

And when I was ready to leave the house, it was my mother who drove me all over Chinatown and Japantown, scoping out Liberty's favored herbalists and tea sellers, then traipsing through Berkeley and Oakland to locate alternative tea merchants. They all knew who she was, and none accepted the news that she had passed easily.

"Drink in her honor," Mr. Fong had insisted, carefully scooping two precious helpings of Kunlun Snow Chrysanthemum flower tea into a pouch.

In my spare time I baked while I poured over her notes.

"Palm leaf-shaped French sugar pastries with lavender." I'd proudly announce as I set my creation in front of my parents. Patty frequently came down to taste test. "Liberty says sugar cookies will marry the notes of chamomile tea. Palmiers are fancier, but I think they will work too."

Dad had been as supportive as he'd promised, more so than I'd expected. "Most parents expect to pay for their child's accommodation when they go away to college," he'd argued. In the end, after working through several scenarios together, I agreed to let them pay for the sixteen-week bread and pastry program and my rent until it was complete.

And for those long months, I busted butt. Yes, I'd chosen a different route than the standard, formal education, but I'd finally found my rhythm. Instead of pouring over books in some college library, I poured over cookbooks and studied the history of tea at the local library. Instead of falling asleep during endless lectures, I received real-life lessons in business negotiations as I haggled, with my father and a great real estate agent at my side, the terms of a lease agreement, and then lessons in architecture and interior design when I had blueprints and plans drawn up. Instead of chained to a desk, I cloaked myself in a white smock and cap, cultivating my skills for my own pastry kitchen.

Now I was here, in this car, on my way to the final lesson before I could open my doors for business. I needed to complete this crucial part of my education, and my healing, before anything else could actually start.

Dad pulled the car up to the curb, checking the window before getting out. He opened Mom's door, then mine, and went to the back to open the trunk.

Mom wrapped her arms around me. She said nothing, just held me tight.

Dad came around with my roller bag, leaving it to stand on the pavement before taking both of us into an embrace. We stood clinging to each other, my parents trying to hold onto the last remnants of their little girl— and me, not ready to be released from the cradle of this, the purest form of love.

We nodded our wordless goodbyes, and I turned to wave before walking through the glass sliding doors.

The counter was easy to find, its white logo with the round, red crane splashed boldly across it. "Where are we flying to today, miss?"

I imagined Liberty in this same spot, being asked this same question.

Setting my passport and ticket on the counter, I was prepared to pick up the torch and carry on the journey. "Kyoto," I replied. "Today, we're flying to Kyoto."

The sweetness of those words filled my mouth, and the first sense of real hope I'd ever felt warmed me to the soul.